FROM THE WORLD OF

KETAMINE RUSH

# DAISY

by Jim Marcus

**October, 2025**

This book is set in Lato Regular 9/13
Titles in Lato Heavy 16/20

Cover:
**DAISY**

by Jim Marcus 2025

ISBN  979-8-9924718-8-5

**WARNING**

This book glamorizes sex, drugs, music, time travel, and a number of other parts of the human experience that may be dangerous in large quantities or if performed incautiously.

■ II PULSEBLACK II

"The world is full of painful stories. Sometimes it seems as though there aren't any other kind and yet I found myself thinking how beautiful that glint of water was through the trees."

**-Octavia Butler**

Parable of the Sower

DAISY

# Previously:

This is a chance to sort of create an exposition here about where our characters have been and what they've been doing, which, to me, sounds suspiciously like keeping tabs on them, almost as though you don't really trust them. I dislike this idea a lot.

Look, people, these are grown ups who do, like all of us, the best they can, really, on a daily basis. Let's reign in both the judgment and the effulgent comma use.

Ok, now Kerys, who is from a small town in the 26th century called Norico, made famous by an electronic music festival that got stunningly out of hand, is a time traveler who, through a series of events that were, and I lean into this, NOT her fault, got trapped back in the early 21st century with a time machine that no longer worked, landing naked, in the above ground pool of a bunch of hippies.

With the help of her intrepid hippies and this one guy with a great ass named Albio and a bald 27th century Dutch speaking Asian woman named Blu Aafjes, which sounds a little bit like how they would write out the sound a sneeze makes in Icelandic, absolutely saved the fucking day by learning how to time travel by getting super fucking high and performing sex acts on each other.

Thusly, they saved the future and taught us a valuable lesson about the nature of the universe.

If this sounds unlikely to you, there is a good chance you won't like this story, either, which is close to being just, really, a retreading of all the same territory, but LOUDER, which is what all sequels are.

DAISY

# 1. PETM

There are six kinds of people in the world. Wait. Seven, There are seven types of people in the world. Seven or eight. I'm not a psychiatrist.

Eight seems like a lot, though. For types of people.

And despite the fact that I'm a huge extroverted slut, I don't know all these kinds of random people. Most people I know are the first kind of people. These are the people that will just be gloriously naked anywhere they can be.

And that's me.

I'm wearing combat boots, because I'm not indestructible, and who knows what kind of prehistoric ick populates the world at this time. Also, everything poops. I think there was a book written about that. I'm real far from a library, right now, though.

So, if that's your look, vagina forward with big-ass boots on, you probably should come on back to the PETM to party. Remember the absence of razors, so imagine all that with a massive unrestrained flowering 70's bush. So, come visit, hang out. Shave me.

Or rescue me or something.

I put my last recording bead in my hand and sent it forward  a few million years. At least that's what it felt like in my head. That wasn't going to cut it. I doubted some early species of lizard was going to find that, get turned on by the idea of a stranded naked future hottie and sidle back here to wine and dine my happy ass back home.

I looked down at the smiling committee of Eohippus prancing around at my feet, too small to ride, too big to safely pet, and stuck out my tongue. Help or get out of the way, tiny horse bitches. One of them, whom I had named "never-ending story", stuck her tongue out back at me. Rude.

Ok, I'm not going to go into detail about why I'm fifty seven million years or so in the past. You can probably understand that sometimes parties don't go the way you expect them to, and you don't get home on time. Let's not belabor that. Why am I here at the start of the Eocene- specifically during the Paleocene-Eocene Thermal Maximum, where temperatures rose dramatically and fifty percent of the existing mammals died out, the rest becoming smaller and bitchier and better equipped to manage the intense heat? Again, that explanation is long and fruitlessly tangential to the point.

The point is that I can't seem to get home. And it's hot.

And I'm very very smart. My name is Kerys. I'm a twenty sixth century physicist, one of a group who figured out, about two years ago (my time) how to travel through time without using expensive machinery. My friends and I had focused on a number of different methods and finally realized that the universe itself had a kind of intentionality- a kind of will. And that will recognized the beauty in it. And was actually sort of proud and willing to bounce you around to play tourist and see it all.

All it took was to recognize the swirly visuals that the universe used to point out its creations, the places to be, the wonders to see.

You really just needed to pay attention. And I was. I promise you. I paid good attention goodly.

But it was becoming clear that the universe had a certain amount of energy at certain times. Energy it could waste ferrying fuckers like me around anywhere we wanted to go. And that sometimes...

Well, sometimes it didn't.

My plan A was waiting to see if the energy increased at any time, allowing me to at least start shifting myself forward, but, after about a month here, it was becoming clear that this wasn't happening,

Luckily, I had been trapped in the past, kinda, before, and I had thought about this problem a lot. I was primed to find a plan B.

Insufferably, French people have a phrase, "Esprit de escalier," which means, "the spirit of the stairwell." Basically, it's "what I should have said back then but I wasn't cool enough." Like when you don't insult someone enough for the situation and you realize later that you just figured out a superior insult. For example, why didn't I name that little horse fucker "Bojack?"

Time travel is usually a great fix for this. You have no idea how many times I've just shuttled back five minutes to insult someone better. I once went ten minutes back to the past three times in a row to enjoy calling a security robot with boobs "Summer Glau," because, yes, it was THAT satisfying. Why would you put boobs on a security robot? This is how I choose to use the most awesome power in the universe.

Or used, because right now, I can't time travel out of a wet paper bag. But still, the French come through. I spent many hours in the figurative stairwell trying to figure out how I would travel forward in time, minus functioning technology. And I landed on a few. Remember, I'm only trying to move FORWARD in time. That is fundamentally different from going backward. This much is made clear by the hastily constructed logic of number one:

**How to move forward in time when the universe is being a little bitch:**

**1. Do not die.**

That's right. I'm already moving forward in time. I'm doing it one minute at a time, just like you are. My minutes are more naked and fun-filled, sure, but it's the same.

I'm not trying to move forward into the future, PER SE. I'm trying to move forward without experiencing the adverse effects of moving forward, some of which include eventual aging, infirmity, and death. Among the others are intense boredom and avoiding fossilization, decay, and carbon dating myself at 57 million years old. So, I'm trying to cheat. So, first way, be immortal and immune to the psychological effects of boredom. And I have the whole world full of resources to work with, including reams of tiny prehistoric horse manure.

## 2. Suspended animation via extreme cold.

We call this one the "Captain America." And sure, it can work. But there are some extreme complications. One of which being, Fuck it's cold. I'm shivering just thinking about it. Luckily, as i mentioned I have a fine bush fully grown in to keep me toasty, but we're talking about getting my body temp down into the liquid nitrogen range, which is about -196 Celsius - super fucking uncomfortable. On top of which, In order to prevent ice crystal formation, which can damage cells, Permeating, penetrating cryoprotectant agents should be used during the freezing process, and distilling dimethyl sulfoxide, glycerol, ethylene glycol, and propylene glycol in an Eocine field using existing materials sounds daunting even if the distant past wasn't making me feel ADHD as fuck. As an aside, if you are going to quote a sentence from all this for a blurb, choose that last one.

## 3. Get a really fat friend.

One of the ways to slow down time is to be in a super intense gravity field. I feel like we've discussed this before. Gravity warps spacetime, causing time to pass more slowly in regions with stronger gravity.

So, just being on big fat earth, we're experiencing time dilation if we compare that to people living on a skinnier planet or off in space somewhere outside of a gravity well. Because gravity isn't really a force, like we usually think of it, but a kind of condition, a curvature, like your weird-ass penis. And that curvature affects everything, even time. We used to use a variation of this, using light to simulate the effects of gravity.

So, I don't have a clock right now, because I haven't bothered to flintstone that shit out of old dinosaur parts, but if I did, our proximity to Earth's gravitational well would cause it to accumulate around 0.0219 fewer seconds over a period of one year than the same fucked up dino clock sitting in space somewhere. So, to be clear, that differential won't cut it.

If you stay completely still and not move at all, the human skeleton can stand gravity incrementals of about fifty or so times Earth's gravity. There actually is a time dilation due to the gravity equation. G is the gravitational constant. M is the mass of the object. r is the distance from the center of the object. And c is the speed of light. I'll save you the suspense. Fifty gravities gets you a time dilation of about 0.9997. This means I'll be knocking about five hundred and seventy thousand years off my trip, plus I won't be able to move. I'll probably also get smushed. Taken all together, that's worse than Spirit Airlines. Moving on.

**4. Go Fast.**

There are some immutable laws of the universe. Human beings have an inexorable desire for bangs until they cut their hair into bangs. This is universal. But it's not the only universal law. The closer I get to the speed of light, the slower my own personal time is going to get.

So, if you strapped on your running shoes and ran at 90% of the speed of light, you would see time going more quickly for the normies around you. Time for them has shifted compared to the same amount of time for you. And like everything fun in the universe, there's an equation for that, too. It's called the Lorentz factor. And all we need to do to work out how much time will dilate at the speed v, is to multiply by this crazy Lorentz factor.

This equation can also be rearranged to give an expression for finding the speed v, at which one would need to travel to get a certain Lorentz factor. In the equation, v is the velocity that someone is moving and c denotes the constant speed of light, while p is for how pretty you are. That last one is not true, but I needed to see if you were paying attention or just zoning out. If we play with the numbers, we see that travelling 99.9999999933% of the speed of light gets us a time dilation ratio of 86,400, which means about one second for every day. Which means I'm traveling for almost 3 days at very nearly the speed of light. And that would work.

Except for this other rule of the universe that says that my mass will increase as I approach the speed of light, meaning it will take more power to move me, meaning that to get to 99.9999999933% of the speed of light, I will need most of the energy ever generated by the universe. In a big 9 volt battery to go. That's a fucking com-ed bill.

Luckily, there is a number 5.

### 5. Do any of these things recursively.

In 2002, Warner Brothers/Dreamworks produced a movie starring Guy Pierce and Samantha Mumba. Jeremy Irons was in it. Oh, and Orlando Jones, before he ran for congress.

It was an uneven movie and it fairly butchered the book, but there was a hint in it, to the 5th way. In the movie,

Pierce, playing the role of a giant Cigar, sits in his time machine and moves into the future. While he's doing that he can see, outside his bubble, time moving superfast for other people. At one point, a bad guy falls partially outside the bubble and that part of him ages superfast. It's gross, but interesting. Basically, it is illustrating an important rule of time itself. Time dilations are specific to the systems they inhabit. So when a condition that causes any kind of dilation is imposed on a closed system that contains that condition, the time changes that result are ALSO contained in that closed system.

Essentially, you can dilate time in a bubble and then when you open that bubble system, the movement of time snaps back to its natural progress.

We all didn't think twice watching that. But the implications are interesting. What if Guy Pierce built a slightly smaller time machine and ran it inside the closed system bubble of the bigger time machine? And what if he put another smaller one inside that one? Again, I'll save you the suspense. It's recursive.

And because of how indulgent the universe likes to be with its exponential multiples, it's extremely fucking recursive.

So maybe I don't need one bubble going 99.9999999933% the speed of light, fluttering back and forth. Maybe what I really need is seventeen bubbles, each sitting inside the other one, each independently fluttering at 89% the speed of light, creating a series of recursive exponential increases in the ratios of time movement.

And instead of using most of the energy of the universe, I can use the admittedly massive energy output of that volcano over there and then each successive bubble can use the kinetic friction energy of the enclosing one (yes, nerds, we lose some to the second law of thermodynamics, but it's not that much, because the whole system is HOT).

And instead of nearly 3 days, Now I only have to travel for about thirty seconds in, again, a very hot bubble. I could add another bubble and go faster, but then I would lose any accuracy and gain five more degrees my hair doesn't need. I'm about 56 million years away from the dawn of coconut oil and while black don't crack, it does frizz.

Now, I need to get my tight little ass to that volcano. Being a little more aware of their own welfare, most of the animals around me were moving, generally AWAY from the volcano. But that lack of concern for my own life in the face of a stupid scientific adventure is what was making me the dominant lifeform on the planet right now, a designation I would probably be giving up by returning to my own time. Probably.

If you stopped right now and did a natural language search on your computer for "can you ride a Hyracotherium (or Eohippus)," the answer will be "no," because even though the little fuckers LOOK like horses and are the distant ancestors of horses, they are only about the size of a large terrier and they will freak out if you tried to ride them and literally shit everywhere.

Because I don't have Bing in the distant prehistoric past, I found that out the natural normal way people find out stuff. Also, if you are dumb enough to try to ride an Andrewsarchus because you think it looks like a big friendly pig, you will be disabused of that opinion quickly. Yes, it's an Entelodont, but it hates you. And no part of it tastes like bacon. Again, experience. So, I walked.

It took me about three weeks to build this thing and it admittedly looked shaky as hell. But the truth was that as long as I got close to home I'd be fine. I just needed to get out of this low energy area into a more reasonable timeline. I felt like I was building a rickety bike that just had to not fall apart or explode until it got me to the river so I could jump in.

And all i had to do was to invent modern metallurgy, modern energy dynamics and not starve to death while doing it.

When it was finished, I named it "Meatball" because that was the first thing I wanted in my mouth when I got home. In all the time I'd been here, the tastiest thing I'd eaten was something that looked like an extremely cute giant bat pokemon with piercing guilt inducing eyes and soft little "don't kill me" human-looking hands. So, I was pretty emotionally fucked up and hungry at this point and just really wanted a piece of meat that didn't make me metaphysically feel bad.

It's remarkably hard to math when you can't write anything down on a piece of paper with a nice modern pencil. But I'm pretty sure this was the working bubble machine that was going to get me home.

I said goodbye to Mr. Ed, Secretariat, Sea Biscuit, Pegasus, and Spirit, stallion of the Cimaron and climbed into the tiny ass little center bubble. There was still enough energy in this time to move things around slightly in time, tiny objects. This had helped me build this thing a lot faster and I used that now to "stitch shut" the bubble with me in it. From inside, the many layers kept me from seeing anything clearly, almost delivering a kind of "frosted" effect, obfuscating the shapes of the objects around me.

I listened for the groan of the volcano and it wasn't long until I heard it. The air got thick and stuffy and I could see red all around me as though the ball had been transplanted inside a living heart. There was a low hum as the sounds of the various levels began, spinning and fluttering.I looked up at the integrity of the internal gyro, struggling to keep the whole thing upright.

The light outside the bubble began to flicker, at first it looked like I could see the days passing, but it seemed uneven, irregular. I steadied myself with a hand on the bubble and the heat was jarring, almost painful. Suddenly I thought back to the pair of shorts that might have insulated my ass, the ones I had shown up in last month, eaten, finally, by a baby Sarkastodon that had, I'm pretty sure, developed a kind of crush on me and just wanted to get my attention. I don't know if I had mentioned that I'm the dominant lifeform on the planet.

I moved away from the slides of the bubble and watched the translucent walls. The light greyed out and went black, a deep and dense velvety black that didn't feel comforting at all. I shifted while my eyes started to get accustomed to the lack of light, trying to do the math in my head for how far I had gone.

Apparently, this was all one more activity than I was prepared to do simultaneously, as I slipped, my boots sliding up the rounded floor of the glass-like bubble and sending me backwards, where I hit my head against the hot inner wall of the machine.

I remember wondering who that robot was in the dark before my eyes closed and the dark got even worse.

## 2. Planeplace

I can't tell you how much I love the word "Meanwhile…" It has chocolatey cinnamon notes of intrigue while being steeped in the savory philosophy of synchrony, where related events are happening simultaneously. But that's just not the kinds of worlds we live in, and I mostly use it ironically. So, here goes:

Meanwhile, while I was trapped in the super distant tiny-horse-having past, Albio was trying to get back home from a trip to Germany. See, that works, even though our personal times are separated by so many millions of years that his species isn't even a glint in the eye of the sperm of the accidental ejaculation of some early horse-faced mammal I have tried and failed to ride more often than I'm willing to admit.

I'm going to make this more exciting by giving you a blow-by-blow of what he is probably thinking, which I feel comfortable doing based on how cloyingly simple he can be and by how often his face has been stashed away in some various parts of my naked places. I may get it wrong here and there because, despite, again, being the dominant  lifeform when I am currently located, I'm only human.

Because I was recently knocked off my ass  and saw a strange robot where it didn't belong as I blacked out. This becomes important at one point.

So, anyway, this was happening.

"I don't understand what's going on, if you don't have my bag, I can file some kind of request thing and you send it to me, right?" Albio was flashing his smile at the girl at the baggage counter, who seemed to be furiously calling, well… other people.

The blonde woman behind the counter couldn't have been more than 24. She gave out those vibes of, "this is above my paygrade," while she tried to smile.

"Sir, it's not that easy, if you give us a twistelekist, we're just trying to mathinka nettikura the issue here."

Albio was thinking he might have misheard a substantial portion of that.

In front of the counter was a girl with a shock of light green hair. She was busily trying to argue with the blonde girl, splitting her focus. Albio could make out that she might have been the blonde girl's roommate or her lover, or possibly her sister or cousin. Her name was "ook" or "fuck" and the blonde girl's name was "Pat" or "slam"

Lip reading is an art, really. Try to follow.

His mind raced through what was in the bag, shrugging as he decided, finally, that he could live without all of it, including the bottle of anti-fungus tea tree shampoo he had bought in bulk a few months back. He had, honestly, not thought about fungus once since he started using it, which is, really, the right amount to think about fungus. He had, like, 20 bottles of it at home, though, an impenetrable plastic wall of defense against fungus. He loved the stuff.

It smelled good, too.

He stepped back over. "If you can't find the bag, I'm ok with it," he smiled at her. The green haired girl smiled at him. Lots of smiling going on here, for nothing happening.

She was not having it. If anything, it seemed to be freaking her out more.

"Can I see that passport again kula?"

She started reaching for his passport. She had looked at his passport five or six times in a panic. Sometimes you wonder if your picture is just shit. Or is it more? And who was Kula?

"I can reach out later." He started to walk away, until she called out after him.

"Just one more twistelekist." He saw her speak into a microphone. And, suddenly, her voice was amplified all over. "Planeplace security, to Baggage check 4."

If I know Albio, he made a little mouth movement repeating the word "Planeplace." That word made no sense. But the word, "Security," did.

He faced forward and began to sort of speed walk to the exit, the kind where your little butt shakes while you move. Luckily, he didn't have any baggage slowing him down. He looked up at the signs. Sure enough, substituting for "Airport," they all said "Planeplace."

I want to go on record, for a second, to state that I've been to some Buddy Holly, jacked up, toothless timelines, but to land on the word "Planeplace" instead of "Airport," is really the sign of some whack naming conventions. Albio shook his head and realized it would probably all go downhill from there.

But why was he in a different timeline? He kept power walking until he sidled up next to a garbage can. Suddenly, there were four men in front of him, in blue suits. He mumbled something under his breath, reaching into the can, and pulled out a black metal rod. He swung it, clocking the closest man in the head. He went sprawling on the floor in front of them as Albio launched himself at the one next to him, swinging the rod upward and connecting between his legs.

That guy went down.. You would, too. Don't lie.

Albio got the third guy in the neck with the metal pole, forcing him to drop to the ground and start choking. The final Guy in blue held his hands up.

"Kobo. Truce, Truce. We just want to mathinka nettikura with your passport." The blonde girl and her green haired Aunt, maybe, came running up behind him.

"What the Cluff, Sergio," Pat yelled at the security guy.

"Bam, it's kula. We'll take care of this. You and Kush step back."

Albio automatically, in his head, adjusted their names. This opened another line of inquiry. In this timeline, were "Bam" and "Kush" just normal human people names? Because no. And, again, who was Kula? This is why everyone hates flying, I, as narrator was forcing him to think.

Albio was breathing hard. "Why do you want to see my passport?"

Sergio looked at him. "Kobo. What's a Germany?"

Albio shook his head. There was no denying he stepped off the plane into a different timeline. But what happened? "You know, you could just ask?"

Kush looked impressed. "Also, kobo, where did you get a black metal pole?"

That was the more interesting question. If you are wondering what a Germany is, too, you are clearly in the wrong timeline to be reading this book and maybe put it down, because shit is about to start moving real fast.

After this.

For the purpose of short jumps, you can consider yourself to be part of the same localized closed system. The universe is pretty forgiving about origination, so subtractionists through history (ha. See what I did there) have developed some personal guidelines that help. This is useful if you need, like, a black metal pole for an airport battle. No. I will not use the word "Planeplace."

**5 Things to remember about your personal localized closed loops:**

**1. Get super chummy with your future self.**

You have to learn to trust future you.

Even if you aren't traveling right now, keep in mind that your future self can reach around and give you a handy sometimes, if you need it. Want one of those 4 cheese reheatable lasagnas? Just remember to buy one later and have future you plop it into the freezer at some point in the past. Does the universe care where it came from or that you are eating it, potentially, before it was shipped from the main office? No.

I had a hamburger once that was delicious, probably about a week before the cow died, because the universe has better things to worry about than where your 3am drunken fourthmeals come from. This leads to:

## 2. Be vigilant in your relationship with past you.

In this crazy world we live in, it's so easy to hate past you Don't do it. Past you is relying on you to keep up any and all you-bargains you have made with this uncaring freakish universe. So you have to follow through on the plans that benefitted you. Did past you get 200 bucks from the future for the happy ending at the massage parlor? Current you is going to have to get 200 bucks, even if it means giving out handies at the massage parlor.

You can force the universe to do ironic shit like that if you're paying attention. Grab someone's wallet at an AA meeting to send back in time so past you can get that third long island iced tea?

Don't keep past you waiting. Even if you don't approve of what they have going on, supporting past you keeps you in the same localized closed system. And that is useful.

### 3. Keep your expectations real

There an old subtractionist saying, "If you've never decapitated anyone, don't rely on future you to procure you a head." I don't know where this saying comes from, but I'm sure it was a lighthearted, drama-free situation that spawned it.

Be reasonable with what you imagine future you is going to deliver. Future you is not magical. Future you is just a person, just like you, in a situation, too. You aren't going to get rich in the next day or so, grow 4 more arms, or learn how to build a car. Regular people problem applies. In a timeline, you are regular people. So is future you. Expanding on that:


### 4. Future you has shit going on, too.

Ok, this should be obvious, but future you may have more complex problems than you, right now. Have you ever noticed that life doesn't really get simpler as the days go on? That's right, it gets more complex. Putting all your faith in future you is deadly. Future you might be in a bit of a bind, too. Hopefully, you are doing your best to keep things easy and fun for future you. If not, stop right now and get some much needed therapy.

Your job is not to make future you miserable and their job is not to rescue you from every possible situation. Be reasonable. A little knife and a cup of water may help you escape being burned alive as a witch. Future you is probably going to be too busy to send back the 51st Division New York Fire Department.

But most of all, remember...

## 5. This is a one way relationship, baby. But it feels like a threeway.

Like many of the best relationships torturing you all through college, this one is one way. And it's not you and some preening debate team star with more ween than wisdom who is mostly interested in you for your flowering newfound ability to line up FFM threesomes, even in your mostly humorless women's studies class. This one favors past you who can start plans, initiate exchanges, etc. That gives past you a unique responsibility, too. Subtractionists are known to leave things lying around in specific places, hide things they may need later, to try and return the favor. If you manage this right, you could walk away with a lifelong friendship between past and future You, one that can keep you alive.

All of this boils down to a kind of three dimensional look at the world. Present you is trying to do right by past you and future you. It's a weird ass polycule, but it works. Present you is putting things in places she HOPES future you needs and she KNOWS past you already needed.

Which is why Albio was about to flick the black metal rod into the past when it was knocked out of his hand and went skitterring across the floor.

"Fuck."

"Look out." Kush decided, apparently, what side she was on, calling out to Albio as hit-in-the-crotch guy sprung forward. Albio slammed his fist into his face and he went down again.

Sergio had his head in his hands. "Kobo." Albio suspected that this meant "Dude."

He was a second away from inventing what was surely going to be an award winning explanation for why his passport was stamped with an imaginary country when everything went red and loud. Red lights dropped from the roof and a loud klaxon-like alarm sounded all over. Albio looked over at Kush and Bam.

They said, simultaneously. "Fuck. Nasis."

"Albio looked confused, which is a look I miss. For reals. "Wait, you have no Germany, but you have Nazis?

"I don't HAVE Nasis. There just ARE Nasis." I'm sure Kush was making a perfectly reasonable point but it was lost when the space in front of them filled up with masked men in black and red uniforms. Albio went looking for his pipe, but it was lost under the baggage carousels.

Sergio yelled out, "Quick. Kidibidi to the bag squiglers."

"Oh, Jesus, man. Tell me that's not what you people call a baggage carousel."

Bam grabbed Kush's hand and ran. "What's a baggage carousel?"

Albio shook his head and considered letting them all die for semantic reasons.

Sorry, that was me.

He looked around. He flipped over a familiar green cafe table sitting in front of him and there was a large automatic gun taped to the underside of the table. Under his breath, Albio said. "Holy shit, future me. Way to escalate."

He untaped the gun and followed Sergio, Bam, and Kush, pointing at the Nasis to cover them. The incoming men were shooting, but didn't seem to have hit anyone yet. The entire area was clearing out ahead of them.

Albio whispered to Bam, "Hey, explain to me like I'm four. What's a Nasi?"

She rolled her eyes, which I think I had programmed him previously to think was adorable. "Nationalized Aggregated Superior Incels. Nasi. They started gabowing women but now they just gabow everything that won't let them cluff them. Which is everyone. Because who wants to cluff that?"

Albio couldn't argue with whatever part of that logic he understood. He nodded.

"Ok. Fuck this. " He stood up and started to lay down what we, in the business call "covering fire." Sergio, Bam, and Kush started moving back toward toward the counter.

They made it to the counter, pulling in one or two other stragglers, including a woman in an electric wheelchair who, really, could have been moving faster. I know that model. Bam flipped a switch and the counter closed up around them into a kind of panic room, black bulletproof glass descending all over. Albio could only faintly see the Nasis run by looking through it. Bam looked over at him.

"Hey, were you trying to shoot them?"

Albio thought for a second. "I think I was." He looked down at the gun. "It must be in stormtrooper mode." Then it hit him. He fired a shot into the air.

"Sonofabitch," Sergio cowered. For a security guy, he seemed deeply insecure. For that and more extraordinary wit, come back to the Eocene era and save me.

"It's ok, man. It's a prop gun. It shoots blanks." He sighed.

Kush's eyes widened. "Mawowzie. where did you get that?"

Albio sighed and pointed it down. Lots of sighing going on, too. "Future me duct taped it to the underside of a Starbucks cafe table"

Kush cocked her head and smiled. "I know, like, three of those words."

He tossed the gun to the counter. It missed and fell. Bam reached over to grab it, under the counter. She called out, "Shit."

"What?" Albio stepped over.

She stood up slowly, holding a sphere a little larger than an egg. It was beeping and blinking faster and faster. "A bomb. Bomb. "

Kush yelled out. "Drop it," as she slammed into the door, followed by the other people behind the panic room counter. Albio pushed the lady in the wheelchair, covering her up a few hundred meters later when the whole thing went up.  It looked like no one went with it.

Albio made a mental note. He now owed his past self a metal rod and a prop machine gun. He sighed.  You don't want to be in debt to your past self. He made his way over to the cafe where he had gotten the gun. It looked like the Starbucks logo, but after closer inspection, it was called "Sturkels Cofey." One "f", one "e" and a "y." Albio hated that. And "Sturkels" sounded like a discount purse shop. Piss on this timeline.

He looked up and saw the black metal rods holding up the green awning and unscrewed the one closest. Blinking for a second, he watched it disappear out of his hand. He turned around and Kush was standing there, fascinated.

"Mawowzie."

He sighed and explained. "I send that back an hour so it would be in that garbage can over there so I could hit that guy in the head with it."

"That's mawowzie"

Albio ran his hands through his hair. It was still blondish brown but it was a bit shorter. He had just gotten it cut. He was still the same handsome Albio I had fucked across the time travelers convention but now he just knew a little more about what was going on.

Usually.

"Now, I just need to find a prop machine gun."

Kush looked around and grabbed his arm, "come on."

People were recovering from the Nasi invasion as they moved down the corridor. Albio saw one or two bodies on the ground, reminding him that this was serious, as he shook his head at the inexpert naming conventions that seemed to permeate this horrible timeline.

He turned to Kush, pointing to a sign, "You know Wankbreads is a terrible name for a pretzel."

"What's a pretzel?"

Albio pointed to the sign again, harder. He pointed superhard. Annie's Wankbreads. "Those"

"Oh. What's the knitkish? It's bread and you wank it around until it's all tied up and stuff. What does Pretzel mean?"

Albio was suddenly at a loss. What DID pretzel mean? Was wankbreads actually a better name for it?"

He put his head down and sighed. "You know where a prop gun is?"

"I do. I am an actor." She looked proud for a moment. "And I am an extra in this period drama. Phony guns everywhere, Fat eyesyearsy in a skyplane cubby right next to the planeplace."

Albio shook his head. The more she talked the more it hurt his head. He tried to switch the subject. "So, you're an actor?"

"I'm an influencer, too. I have a show on masturbation station you've probably kloddied it."

Albio closed his eyes. "Of course the word "Influencer" was the same.

"What's masturbation station?"

She stopped and felt her pockets. "One sec. My eyesyearsy" she said, shifting it to landscape mode. It looked like Masturbation Station was a kind of onlyfans site in this timeline. She played a video that showed her and a pretty black girl with wild hair kissing naked in a hot tub.

In the video, Kush stood up, naked, and slid down the black girl's body, pulling her up to sit on the edge of the hot tub before burying her face in her bush. Another dark-haired girl sat naked at the edge of the tub splashing.

"Did you just call your phone an Eyesyearsy?"

"What's a phone?" Kush stared at him.

That was actually not what Albio was focusing on at the moment, though.

"I think that's my girlfriend's bush."

## 3. Pocalypse Cow

I want you to imagine the earth at the end. So, this is when the people are mostly gone. Sure, some of those people looking to sell you fucked up car insurance are still there. But they have mostly become mutates, mindless husks walking the earth, looking for food, sick with the long terms effects of ancient radiation-filled war skies their descendants invoked, breeding forever less and less true, dying slowly across the plains of a planet no longer capable of sustaining even their meager efforts at life.

Blah blah blah. You've seen it before in movies. It's really pretty gross. The problem is that this is always a time of desolation, but, more to the point, it's a time of pus. Everything seems so pus filled. Mutates? Full of pus.

You've seen it.

But you probably didn't see this. There is a middle eastern looking woman with long black hair, under a cropped black long sleeve hoodie sweater, a tiny pair of faded blue jean shorts and boots running through the field holding something close to her chest. She slams into the first of the mutates, leaving a hole in his chest that he seems to not notice. Spinning deftly, She knocks over another who explodes on the ground like a greenish pink balloon filled with pus.

So much pus.

Then, with one arm, she neatly severs the head of another one as she dives past him, her precious cargo still intact in her arms.

She makes it a few yards further and jumps in the air, opening her arms and slamming the object to the ground and cheering.

"Eat me, motherfuckers! Eat my dick!" She yelled, the football bouncing through the air.

She wooted some more and then did a karate kick to another ambling mutate, knocking his head off and sending him sprawling backward.

Her name is Vietta and she is my natural born enemy. My archnemesis. Fine, yes, she is the best football player on earth right now, but slim pickens on that one and it's millions of years since the last draft, so…

To explain this, I may have to go back and explain who we are. Vietta and I and Albio are part of a group known as subtractionists. As you might infer from the title, our jobs are to go through time and remove the ugly shit that makes people miserable. We train to do that. The center for where the subtractionists do their work is in the 23rd century, which is when the idea was sort of invented, so Albio, being from the 21st century, is sort of an outlier. That one was my fault. Vietta and I, however, are from the 26th century and we trained together.

Which is the problem.

Subtractionists are usually pretty easy going people. Mostly because of something we call "Question 1." You see, there are lots of things that make for a great subtractionist, or "Rat" as we call ourselves, but the number one thing all of us have to have, is the ability to have fun no matter where we are. Why is that, you ask?

Well, I'll tell you, imaginary person.

In our line of work, it's almost invariable that we will get stuck somewhere in some timeline needing to not fuck anything up and have to just stay there. The people in charge wanted to make sure that, in that extremely likely event, we would be happy just ditching all our high tech gear and dressing like a local, sinking into the modern day music streaming playlists, and behaving.

Which is why this crazy bitch was somewhere toward the end of the global apocalypse, playing American football with a bunch of human mutates. And, yes, she was MVP, but, really, look at the competition.

And there's that word.

The problem was that Vietta LOVED competition. And despite being one of my best friends and most amicable naked time-travelling fuck buddies at the beginning of our training, her drive to compete with me turned her into my most dreaded and horrific evil enemy by the end.

Evil

Am I happy she's seemingly trapped here at the end of the apocalypse? Maybe. Do I understand why? No. Is that pissing me off, more than you can possibly know? You don't know me as well as you will by the end of all this, but I like to have answers.

So, Vietta kicked a few more mutates to death until she felt bad enough to walk back to her little house. Behind a big ass copper statue she had a wooden and plastic cabin, along with a small pen on the side where she had managed to collect the one or two animals left that didn't look too sick to one day eat. This, for her, meant 2 frazzled goats and a three legged cow, constantly at risk of tipping her own self over.

Sometimes Vietta liked to lean against the ragged homemade fence, made of wood with black rusted wires wrapped through it to hold it up, and stare at her balding, raggedy, threadbare trio of animal monstrosities, imagining a new world rising from the anemic ashes of this petrified infirmity, to reclaim the earth, spreading beauty and life once again across its bilious face.

It was at this exact moment that her cow exploded.

Am I sad that my makeshift time machine appeared inside what was likely the last cow on earth, spraying nearly the entirety of its mass of pus infested blood and fragments of bone and organ pieces all over Vietta as a thin layer of brownish red goo that smelled only vaguely of steak tartar?

That's a two part question. Sad about the cow, which she had named, optimistically, T-Bone, but not sorry about the rest.

Couldn't have happened to a nicer bitch.

My eggshell thin 17 layer deep makeshift cobbled-together Paleocene-Eocene era time machine was dissolving amidst the cow detritus like on overcooked manchego cheese ravioli in a glass pint of hydrochloric acid. I had missed most of the extended trip due to being unconscious and now was busily climbing out of the sloppy high-tech uterus swimming in my own 60 million year old juices wishing I'd been conscious enough to hit the big red "off" button 5 minutes earlier.

But we all have regrets.

I looked up to see Vietta standing over me, more in need of a shower than I was and mouthed, "Oh, fuck me."

She stared down at me in disbelief.

"No fucking way."

I looked up, pleased to see a human being, yet simultaneously let down by the universe's choice of human being to be making me see. If that makes sense.

"You look good."

"Go fuck yourself, Kerys, that was my last cow."

I sniffed. "It smells like it might have gone bad?"

"Yeah, it went bad. We're in the apocalypse, bitch." She halfheartedly helped me up. I would pay for that later. This gave me the chance to review her outfit, which I confess, despite the fact that it looked like someone had dipped her in the tomato gravy on the one side like a fresh piece of garlic bread, was cute af. She looked me over, too, noticing the unkempt and courageously outre appearance of my bush, probably since it was literally the only thing I had on outside my boots.

"Do you need a razor, you crazy cow-popping cunt?"

"Yes. Yes, I do, Vietta, because I was trapped in the prehistoric past with nothing to keep me company but a bunch of early pre hominid unridable piece of shit little ungroomed horse-faced mammals."

"Well, boo hoo, cuntwaffle, I'm currently trapped in the distant future surrounded by ambling human shaped organ bag mutates while unshaven cheating death bitches eviscerate my fucking livestock."

"Maybe your cow should have been a little smarter and not been right where my admittedly masterfully designed improbably constructed time machine was destined to appear."

"Maybe fuck you in the asshole, you thicc sweaty-titted bitch, the joke's on you because they don't make smart cows in any timeline, which you would know if you ever did your own fucking homework."

This was clearly getting us nowhere. I grabbed on to the only pertinent information I had taken from her crazed and witless tirade.

"My tits do look good."

"Why are you here, Kerys?"

I shook it off and started walking toward what looked like her cabin. If anything, it was a degree or two hotter here at the end of the earth than it was at the dawn of the planet. I had completely slept through the reasonably temperate and responsibly air conditioned 60 million years in between and that, suddenly, pissed me off a lot. I shook my head vigorously and pined for a shower. "To rescue you." I hadn't considered it, but, sure, if I rescued myself, I could take her with, if she wasn't being too much of a knob.

Vietta followed me, stomping as heavily as she could make those spindly little baby legs stomp. "Or to make me rescue you, probably."

I turned to her and said, calmly and reasonably, "You couldn't rescue a buttplug out of your own unibomber looking ass, you shifty fucking clit."

"Yeah, well, you were trapped twice. I'm only trapped once, cowbomber." She waved two fingers in my face, manically. "Twice."

I looked up to see a giant bronze statue in front of her modest cabin. It had the words "Kerys sucks" spraypainted across it and bore a loose, easy-going, yet insulting resemblance to me."

"Holy shit, Rectum, where did you get a statue of me?"

Vietta stepped over. "Get over yourself. It's actually Gloria Gaynor." She reached over and pushed a button I hadn't noticed on the base. A tiny recording blared out.

*At first I was afraid, I was petrified*

*Thinking I could live without you by my side*

*And after spending nights*

*Thinking how you did me wrong*

*I grew strong*

*And I learned how to get along*

*Now you're back*

*From outer space*

*And I find you here*

*With that sad look upon your face*

*I should've changed that stupid lock*

*Or made you leave your key*

*If I'd've known for a second*

*You'd be back to bother me*

*Go on, go, walk out the door*

*Turn around now*

*You're not welcome anymore*

*You're the one who tried to hurt me with goodbye*

*Think I'd crumble?*

*You think I'd lay down and die?*

*No, not I, I will survive*

I nodded, "That's uplifting, actually."

"Kept ME going." Vietta took a breath. "Bitch."

We made our way to her cabin. It was mostly something out of Hoarders, fort knox edition. She had been stockpiling gold, currency, silver bars, anything of value.

"What the fuck, McDuck?"

"I'm going to get out of here at some point. I'll probably need money where I go. The bills are useless." She handed me one. It said, at top, "Vespuciland," and was, apparently worth "20 shurklets"

"What's a Vespuciland and who are the shurklets?"

"This timeline. It's fucked. In my timeline, right now, in history, it's a paradise. This is San Francisco, United States, in the middle of the biggest space cadet training program in the world. In this timeline, It's the apocalypse in the middle of Blompi, Vespuciland, and you can buy cofey - that's one f, one e, and a y - using shurklets. Not dollars. If you can find a Sturkels, which is... Nevermind."

I stuck out my tongue. It was hard to listen when she looked like the parmigiana version of herself.

Meanwhile I had sweated out everything I'd drunk since 1979 and I could feel it all over me.

"Hey, any chance we can find a shower?"

She rolled her eyes at me, forcing me to realize that, yes, it was as effective a gesture as I had thought. "Yeah, we're going to have to go into town. But I was about to anyway."

She grabbed a bag and threw a bunch of gold bars and cash into it, tossing it over her shoulder. I followed her out of the front door. There was a path in front of her house and we started down it, taking a left at the fork in front. Sure, enough, it looked like there was a small town up about a kilometer ahead.

The path was littered with the occasional ambling post human monster. I figured I'd make conversation.

"Zombies?"

"Nope. Mutates. They're harmless. They're soft. You can kill one if you look at it too hard. And they're all herbivores. Their teeth barely work so they survive eating grass and each other's shit.

I nodded. Ladies and gentlement, the human race.

She went on. "There are about 7 people left- humans- and they all suck." She wiped her face off as best she could and shook it on the ground.

"No offense, Maybe you're not the best judge of character, right now, hoodiepuss."

She sneered, "see for yourself, flatbush, we're about to meet one of them. Unless you don't want a shower."

Honestly, the thought of not showering was making my butt twitch so I followed. "I've been trying. There isn't enough energy here, either, is there?"

"Very observant, vulva. Maybe you can tell me, oh miraculous inventor of new travel? All I know is that if I had a harness I'd be back in my Condo's private swimming pool doing naked laps for the guy in 4G."

I looked down. That one will take a lot of unpacking. About two years ago, my time, My group of weirdos and I invented a new way of traveling through time that didn't require expensive machinery, relying on the energy of the universe. So, no more time harnesses. I hadn't anticipated that there would be periods in the universe where the energy needed to travel was gone. Like now. It made me wonder why. Something she just said made me realize why.

"You like to swim naked for him?"

"Yes, Kerys. Other people besides you have sex."

"That's not... I was thinking. Energy. To swim. From being watched."

"I can swim if I'm not being watched."

"But you don't." It made perfect sense now. I stopped and turned to her. "You said there are like seven people and a bunch of mutates on the planet. Clearly, since I may have obliterated the last cow, there aren't many animals..."

"Clearly."

"So, there is virtually nothing around to observe. To see the universe. Observation has power. This is where the power comes from, to drag motherfuckers around time. The universe seeing itself and realizing it's beautiful. It needs something that can observe."

"Like, people, humans? That's really anthropic." She shook her head.

"No, no, anything. Like I used to use the idea of a Peacock. Not sentient, but willful. It just has to know its being looked at..."

"And know it's looking." She shifted the bag on her shoulder.

"Exactly." We entered the town in front of us.

The ground was glass covered in sand and if I had been wearing normal shoes it might have been slippery as fuck. The buildings just started out of nowhere as though we were entering in the middle of a city.

I looked at one of the first buildings we saw. On it was a symbol drawn with red paint. It looked old, but so did everything else.

"Is that a Donny Darko rabbit- head?"

Vietta shook her head, looking preoccupied. "Who the fuck knows in this messed up timeline."

It definitely added to the post apocalyptic vibe. I flashed the drawing a thumbs up and kept walking.

About two blocks later, she stopped and pointed.

"There."

I looked over. It looked like a motel. The sign on it said "Dip's Sit and Sleep.

"What the fuck is a sit and sleep?"

Vietta sighed heavily, "it's what people here call a motel. Don't lose the plot."

"Oh that really sucks." I followed sullenly.

"Get used to it." She walked into the front door and I followed. The man behind the counter looked to be about 60 years old. He was pale with white hair, wrangled into a faux hawk and a bunch of chains around his neck and waist, but otherwise, he was as naked as I was.

Vietta pretended to smile, "Hey, dipshit, is my thing still safe in the basement?"

He looked us over and nodded. "It's just Dip. And yes. Don't blow anything up. Who's your friend?" He nodded his head at me. I looked over and noticed that he had one of the biggest dicks I had ever personally seen outside an exhibit. He smiled at me and helicoptered a little. I grimaced.

"My sister. She sucks. We need a room for an hour, now, too, to freshen up."

He looked over at her. She looked like Frankenstein had brought a half melted strawberry shortcake ice cream bar to life and then, horrified by his own hubris, had beaten it back to death with a crowbar.

I looked good.

"Yep. that'll be a hundred million Shurklets."

She put the bag on the counter, "Deal. Do you have any towels in the room?"

He looked at her as if a full grown orange tree had sprouted from her head and given birth to the baby Jesus. "There's water, bitch."

I glanced over to see a lost and found box. "We'll grab something from there."

The white tripod started to say something, but I heisted a handful of stuff from the box without looking and followed Vietta up the stairs.

"Do you think Dip blew up the whole planet so he could walk around naked in the apocalypse with his gigantic babyarm dick out?"

"Yes, Kerys, I think that's exactly what happened."

"Fiend." I said.

She pushed open the door and moved over to the sink, pulling her clothes off. I looked through the pile of stuff I'd grabbed and found a plaid washcloth.

"Hey, look. It's a tiny towel." I tossed it to her.

She shook her head sullenly, now completely naked. "You suck."

I smiled, "I heard, sis. Go get clean."

She moved into the shower area while I looked at the room.

It was surprisingly decent. Truthfully, I hadn't been under a real roof in over a month, so I should probably hold off on my Zagats review. I found a bright yellow sundress that was about 2 sizes two big for me and a piece of rope I could wrap around it. So, I was set. Feeling low maintenance, I leaned back and listened to Vietta shower through the thin bathroom wall.

I closed my eyes for a second. When I opened them, she was straddling my face, bottomless, looking down at me. I felt her knees pushing down on my arms as she slid her pussy over my mouth. I opened my lips and licked at it, feeling the redness of her swollen clit. She moved back and forth, filling my mouth up with her. I sucked at her, digging my tongue inside her and then swirling it around her little knob. She pressed down harder on my face and I bit her lips, aggressively pulling her into my mouth, pushing my face upward.

I moved my tongue faster and faster over the tip of her cunt, focusing on her clit, handling it roughly with my lips and tongue. I remembered our time training together, at first, how she would jump on me like this and not let go until I could make her cum on my tongue. I opened up widely and sucked in her entire pussy, letting her juices fill my mouth while I immersed myself in it, got lost in it.

I tongue fucked her hile she rocked back and forth, letting it slip as far as possible into her spaces. She leaned back and my tongue slid into her asshole, pushing in deeply, filling her from behind. She grabbed my hair with both hands and rode my face, covering my mouth by alternating between the tiny hole of her ass and the slippery, liquid hole in front. I tried to let my lips and tongue open and form themselves to her bottom, licking and sucking at her everywhere.

Finally, I could hear her breathing deepen as I sucked at her clit like a tiny dick, the way I used to all those years ago, and was rewarded by the thin drizzle of her cum dripping into my mouth. She rolled over and flopped next to me, still breathing hard.

"I was imagining you were my sister." She laughed.

I shook my head. "That is really fucked up."

"Bitch, I've been in westworld for 3 months. My vibrator died a month ago. Take one for the team." She stood up and I could see she had washed her crop hoodie sweater. She was wearing only that and her boots and was looking around, clearly, for her jean shorts. I was holding onto the yellow sundress. How long was I asleep?

Then the explosions started.

We jumped up and moved to the door. I looked out the eyehole of the door and saw there was a part of the hallway missing.

"Fuck." I took a deep breath and pulled open the door. We bolted into the hallway. Moving down the stairs, we could see that most of the motel was falling to pieces. Fauxhawk was shooting at something right in front of the building, through a window that used to be there.

I looked out the hole and saw what looked like a bunch of desiccated pus bag post humans riding massive mutated elephants, shooting futuristic energy weapons at an elderly naked punk porn star. I turned to Vietta.

"You said they were herbivores."

"Do you see them eating meat right now?" she blinked at me more than was necessary.

She turned and started running down the stairs to the basement. I followed. I've been doing way too much of that shit.

She ran down the hallway to a locked door. Reaching down, she realized she wasn't wearing any shorts. "Sonofabitch."

I ran up behind her and put my boot through the door, knocking it off the hinges. The noises above us got louder. She flicked on the light and I could see it.

It was a retro looking clear-domed time machine.

"Why..." I started.

"Yes, I built a time machine. No, I haven't used it yet. Yes, it might kill me. No, I can't operate it alone. Capisce?"

"Are you Italian now?"

She looked frazzled. I, of course, was calm and well maintained, ready for any eventuality. Still, she continued to bark orders.

"Kerys. Focus. I have to start it. It has an internal battery. But then, when it's ready to go, you need to pull that breaker switch, sending all the power from the grid here, while I press the intake button. Then you run back, close the door, and we leave. Comprende?"

"Stop throwing in random foreign closing words just to suggest I'm not understanding you. I understand you. This isn't rocket science."

"It's…" She screamed for a moment, above the din of the explosions upstairs, then ran to the device. I moved over to the breaker switch. "Are you ready?"

"I'll ask you when you're ready." She was flustered, trying to turn the thing on. I calmly rolled my eyes.

She called out. "Ok, ready?"

"I already said… ok, yes, fine."

The next minute or so blew by pretty quickly. She started the machine and I flipped the switch, diving into the open door. I slammed it shut and the room disappeared. We watched the centuries pass in reverse as the machine slid back into the past seamlessly before coming to a halt, half buried in what looked to be a suburban backyard.

I pushed open the door and crawled out, dragging Vietta after me. I was still holding the yellow sundress while she had managed to retain her black cropped hoodie sweatshirt. But besides that, and two pair of boots, we were naked. The job was probably to find a place inside.

Vietta pointed to a garden house right behind us and we both stepped over to it. The door was open.

Right past the foyer was a wide open area, surrounded by lights. That wasn't the interesting part.

"Fuck me, is that a hottub?"

For those of you that can't see, yes, it was one. And it looked amazing. We pulled off our boots and slid into it. Vietta slithered out of her hoodie sweater thing and threw it in the corner.

If you've ever gone a month without a shower, I can't explain to you what a hot tub might feel like in that situation. So, honestly, I can't tell you how long we were in there, not talking, not moving, not doing anything. Just floating like two Matzoh balls in a tin of chicken soup on some deli warmer, waiting for the lunch rush.

Until a girl with light green hair walked in, crossed her arms, and said, "Hey, what are you glissas doing in my waterbubblecup?"

DAISY

## 4. Punks in the Waterbubblecup

"Also, where is Kush?" Vietta stood up and looked around. Her tits bounced hypnotically. These were good tits on a bad person. It happens.

I pulled her back down into the water. "She's at the Planeplace breaking up with her..."

I looked through the abridged wordmurkle that Kush had brought out from the house. For the third or fourth time, I wished it were indexed by actual normal human people words in this morphosemantic nightmare world. "Galbuddy?"

"Does that mean girlfriend?"

"Yes, sort of," I responded.

Vietta sat back and looked up, kicking at the water. "Elaborate."

"Well, it can also mean someone who you are close with but not smashing. Like "Hey, galbuddy."

"What's the point of that?"

"Look, I'm just the translator. Don't make me know shit." I sank back into the hot tub. I refused to call it a waterbubblecup. Although I could see the etymology of that one clearly.

"A wordmurkle is a dictionary," She said, into the air.

"Yes. Again."

Veitta sunk under the water and returned. "Sorry, hot water makes me stupid."

I literally had a thousand responses prepped for that. "Is that camera still running?" I squinted to see if I could see the red light.

Vietta was humming "I will survive" under her breath. "Probably."

My eyes widened. "The whole time?" For context, we'd been floating around in the hot tub for two weeks, alternating hatefucking each other along with various randos and learning how the word god had fucked this timeline directly in the wet open ass.

"I think we're some kind of erotic internet sensation." She sank under the water again.

I nodded. "Nice." It had been a little bit since I was a meme. I waved my tits at the camera. I leaned back and waited for her to come back up again. A nagging voice in the back of my head said something indecipherable. Or maybe I wasn't listening. Either way, the result was the same. A complete and blissful lack of self awareness.

At that moment, Kush walked in, pulling someone in behind her. "Hey, kobos, I think you know this glurka?"

I squealed. It was Albio. I stood up as he ran to the hottub. I melted all over him.

"Jesus, woman, you're like a raisin." He laughed.

Kush laughed and stripped. "They've been in there for thirteen days. Wait. Where's the other one."

I reached down and pulled Vietta up. She reached her hand out to Albio. "Nice to meet you."

I pulled his shirt off and he stripped naked, jumping in with a splash. Kush, now nude, too, slid in with us. I dragged Albio over by the dick, using it like a handle. "I'm so glad you're here and I didn't have to get out of the water to get you."

He leaned in to kiss me. "Is this where we live now?"

I kissed him. "Yes." Watch out for the Eyesyearsyfat."

He nodded, kissing me deeper, "What the fuck is that?"

I pointed to the camera and waved. He kissed me again. Kush waved, too. "It's my masturbation station channel. I got bumped up to Masturbation Nation because of you guys. I'll probably win a handsy."

Albio breathed into my face. I missed the warmth of his breath on me. He sighed. "I fucking hate this place."

"Agreed." I pulled him back down and cuddled, trying to ignore the camera.

Albio started, "So, I'm in this timeline against my will. And I'm guessing you two didn't come here on purpose?"

I shook my head. "Nope. And this is Vietta?"

His eyes widened. "Wait. THE Vietta?"

I should explain that Albio and I had been together a lot during the last two years, and some of that was actually spent talking. So he had heard many of my stories about Vietta, who was, as I mentioned earlier, my archnemesis. Really, more of a supervillain.

Kush was interested, too. She twirled a little in the water and asked, "Why is she a THE?"

I answered, "Because she's a horrible monster."

Kush was confused, "But didn't you two Cluff my nexty together right in this waterbubblecup two days ago?"

Albio winced, "Is that fucking? Cluffing?"

Vietta and I nodded vigorously, "I know. It's bad. It's a bad word."

Albio shook his head to suggest that this timeline was really disappointing him. He reached under the water and fingered me.

I didn't want to know what THAT was called here. I spread my legs a bit and bore down, smushing his hand under me like an overripe banana under a hot girl's sloppy wet hot vagina. I'm going to come back to this moment later for a better analogy.

He continued. "I threw up in my mouth a little. Was his name Cliff?"

Vietta shook her head. "It's Chris. Regardless, it's a terrible word." She sunk below the water again like an enemy submarine torpedoed by brave allied forces.

I looked over at Kush. "She's still the enemy, just not all her parts all the time. Besides, it's a long story."

Kush giggled. "I like that. Not all her parts."

Albio explained, "In subtractionist training, they used to sort of crib off each other's work and one day Vietta gave her a fake essay and Kerys failed the class and had to take it over again."

Vietta rose back up, like a misshapen humpbacked whale lifting its grey, massive deformed shape above the sheltering waters to spray rotting, decrepit ancient seawater from its festering, torn blowhole. "Actually, she copied off of me over and over again, so I fought back and made a phony essay."

"Did I say the whale thing out loud? I can. whale." I leaned into Albio's hand, trying to really get it up there. I hope that by the time you read this that this is called "Muppetting" and I get credit for it. He muppetted me.

Kush looked at us, "ooh, what was the essay about?"

So, here. This wouldn't have been a big deal for me except it was a big essay. I should probably explain the core points of it.

### How do divergent times work? A study in 5 points.

**1. You can change things in your small, localized environment.**

Just like leaving a gun taped under a cafe table for earlier use, you can change your local timeline in small ways. Time is super forgiving. If you are just adjusting things and then making sure they are consistent, it doesn't care. Time is like a substitute teacher. If no one in class is actively stabbing a cheerleader in the eye, it just sits there and reads its romance novel, eats an apple, and pretends everything this job pays real people money. Any version of you can change time without making major impacts, past you, present you, future you. Like when past me told that Chris guy I'd suck his dick again if he brought me that bottle of champagne I stashed behind the plant right there.

This is important if you absolutely need to return to your own timeline. There was a 20th century torture device invented that was so effective that we still reference it for analogies in the 26th century. You can move an image around a little bit in Microsoft Word and everything is cool. But don't move it too far.

**2. If you change something really important, you will be making a new timeline**

And just like in Microsoft Word, you can drag that picture to the wrong place and suddenly, everything changes. Bam, you are in a new timeline. Imagine that clippy is hanging over your shoulder, content to let you fuck with little shit. Then, at one point, it's like, "Hey, it looks like you are trying to make a new timeline, and rather than ask you to click yes or no, it just does that shit. So now, moving forward may put you in that timeline's future, not your original ones. This doesn't sound hard except...

### 3. You don't decide what's important, the universe does.

Butterfly effect, whatever, some things are important. Some things aren't. But that is not up to you. It's up to the universe. And it might think that the color of your underwear is important today because it impacts some other decision. So, honestly, it's best not to wear any. That sounds stupid, but it is a point.

When traveling, keep variables to a minimum. If this resonates to you like a new excuse to be naked, trust me, I've tried to use it. You have to sort of try to think like the universe does if you want to figure out what to change and what not to change. Which, if you've ever tried to think like an intentional but nonsentient ongoing massive multithreaded event is hard. Your guess is as good as mine, really. The result of this is simple.

### 4. You can't really change your own timeline, but you can influence it.

This is the core of what we do and how it impacts the universe. Let's say I take the cure for cancer, invented in the early 22nd century, and I bring it back a hundred years, as I've done many many times. What happens? Well, first of all, no matter what timeline you are from or what you think, you save billions of people. You end up making a new timeline, but it's still a billion real people. If that's not enough for you, time to hang up your good guy card. That's a literal fuckton of people, Marco.

But here's where the seduction comes in. The universe works in a kind of statistical way. Timelines have a kind of "gravity" where they pull at each other. If you abolish cancer in enough timelines, it sort of pulls other timelines, especially new ones, in that direction.

So, even in your own timeline, you might see things adjusting a bit. Maybe cancer was eradicated a little earlier. Maybe not. If it's too many timelines, we learned a couple years ago, you get what's called a confluence and it pulls all the realities together. That's bad. But for a few timelines, we whimsically call this timeline seduction. But even if you make a major change…

**5. It takes timelines a while to realize something is important.**

So, here's the thing. Even if you make a change that the timeline considers really important, it takes the universe a little bit to realize that. The amount of time varies, but it's often your time to return to your existing future timeline. So let's say you go back in time and teach your mom how to cook. We've all thought about it. If it's a major change and, for some of us it would be, you have a window in which you can get back to your existing timeline, If you miss it, you show up in a timeline where your mom is a great cook, but it's not your timeline.

If you make it, though, in the window, you end up in a timeline that is not very different at all. If you do that a lot, though eventually, your own timeline may have a version of your mom that decided to put more attention into cooking years ago. Your timeline was seduced. Sounds hot.

Kush giggled again. "I love your lists."

I looked at Albio. He laughed. He was opening up the bottle of champagne I had bartered for so expertly. "Yeah, you said that out loud again."

Vietta came bouncing back with glasses she had gotten from the kitchen and climbed back in. "Your neighbors seem cool."

Kush took a glass. "What's a neighbor?"

Albio poured champagne in all the glasses. "So, how long can we stay here?" He handed a glass to Kush.

She took it. "As long as you want. We probably all have to cluff each other every couple of hours to keep up my scorio."

Albio dropped his head and looked at me.

I took a glass. "A scorio is like a ratings. We have to fuck every once in a while for the camera while we sit here and figure shit out. Not a bad deal. I get you next." I finished the glass and handed it back. I should have sucked both of Chris' dicks and gotten two bottles. Did Chris have two dicks? Maybe. I didn't understand any of the shit rules of this timeline.

Vietta made a point to sip hers slowly. "That seems gratuitous. I get him after."

Albio took a drink. "We need more guys."

Vietta nodded and then looked concerned. "You know. I'm almost afraid to ask how he landed here. Serendipity express."

Albio nodded. "I was thinking that."

I tried to process all that. "What are the chances that three subtractionists have all been diverted to the exact same semiotically challenged timeline at various times, ending up together?"

Vietta nodded, "Yeah, I assume that the 'sit and sleep' was the godforsaken future of this horrible place."

Kush pouted. "Hey, this is my kurple."

I grabbed her and pulled her over, kissing her. "You see, that's not a real word. I'm drowning you now." She giggled while I pushed her under, playing with her tits.

Albio sat up on the edge of the hottub. It made it easier for me to lean over and put his cock on my mouth. He fucked my face with his hand in my hair and continued.

"I'm almost afraid to turn on the tv, here, not just because the words will make my head hurt, but also because there is something serendipitous happening and I'm afraid I'll see my mom or something."

"Eek. boner-kill, right?" Vietta poured another glass of champagne down her facehole.

At least that's what I imagine she did. I was too busy sucking this dick in front of me. I buried my face in his balls and wrapped my arms around his ass, trying to get it as far down my throat as it would be. I stretched my neck and leaned forward a bit so I could deep throat it while trying to listen to the conversation.

Kush was back up, undrowned. "What does _____ mean."

Albio was trying to explain the serendipity express. This is when the universe creates a few too many coincidences in order to manage the behavior of time travelers mucking shit up. It's like when the substitute teacher thinks he understands the lesson plan and repeats it over and over. Stuff happens that is not really probable. Possible, but not likely. Like all of us ending up in the same hottub.

Vietta was playing with my tits and rubbing my clit from behind. I spread my legs and kept sucking. I could tell that Albio's explanations were getting weaker as I pumped his dick with my mouth. I could also feel how wet Vietta's fingers were inside me, a different kind of wet than the hotttub. Which gave me an idea. I pulled myself up onto Albio's lap. I reached in my pussy and felt the slick oily wetness, digging my fingers in and rubbing it into my ass. I positioned my asshole over his cock and pointed my cunt at the camera, sliding his prick into my open ass. I slid down slowly. It felt so good.

He reached around and held my tits, kissing my neck as his rod slipped up inside me, filling me up. I grabbed Vietta by the hair and pulled her face into my bush, trying to fuck myself with it.

I hatefucked her pretty face while Albio sunk himself deeper into my asshole. I admit that I let out a stream of dirty talk designed to get him to explode all wet and hot up my hole.

I begged him to destroy my tiny asshole, insisting that he pump his slick cum deep inside my crack while I told Vietta to stick her face in my superior cunthole. I called her every name I could, forcing her dirty dyke face to suck my tiny fat goddess dick, hard up inside her mouth while I bounced on the cock I loved so much until I felt him shake and pour himself right up my waiting ass. It felt warm, even after the hottub, hot, like I had a hot wet towel inside me wiping away all the bullshit from the distant past and distant future, leaving only right now, with someone I loved exploding inside me, taking me, making me part of him.

I came into Vietta's mouth, realizing too, that maybe I didn't hate her that much. Maybe if she did that a few more times.

I reluctantly slid off my favorite prick while Kush, still naked, rolled in a tv cart and plugged it in.

Albio sighed. "Let me guess. That's a shmukie."

Kush looked at him confused. "It's a flickermaker. Don't you have these where you come from?"

It was a large television, if a bit thick and heavy. Nothing seemed really terribly well built in this timeline. And absolutely nothing was terribly well named. An alarm went off behind her and Kush jumped up and down, her breasts geometrically rotating like dual planets in the same gravity well, creating a spatial curvature uniquely their own.

"Guys. That little ass-cluff threeway just got me Masturbation Nation teal level."

I cocked my head. "Is that good?"

She nodded. "Ima make so much Shurklet. I'll share."

Vietta reached for the remote. "You keep your shurklets, babe. We whore for fun." She flicked the television on and started moving through the channels. I grabbed the remote and leaned out of the hottub. She slid behind me and started licking at Albio's balls.

Most of the channels were pretty dull.

I clicked, trying to view each one long enough to check for...

For what? I didn't even know what I was looking for.

Until I saw it.

"Hey, guys."

Vietta turned around. She had been trying to get her tongue up Albio's ass for the camera. Hey, we had to pay for all this hot water somehow. But what I had found on tv was almost as interesting.

Kush looked, "is that..."

It did seem to be a giant mouse, cute af, panicking and crushing people in its wake.

Albio summed it up. "Sonofabitch."

I looked over at Kush. She looked panicked. Is that here?"

She nodded. "Not far."

I tried to process the scene. There was a smaller figure chasing the mouse. I tried to get a good look at it. I looked at the remote. "Hey, does this thing zoom in?"

Kush shook her head, "Have you ever seen a flickermaker?"

She was hot but useless. I got out of the tub and moved toward the tv. I got closer. I turned to look at Albio. "It's Los. It's fucking Carlos. Chasing a giant mouse."

Albio pursed his lips. "So, I vote- not a coincidence."

## 5. Practical Mouse Wrangling

Vietta and I were formally issued a couple of pairs of jean shorts from Kush's massive rock star closet. This is how we all three appeared in the middle of Blompi square, dressed in matching jean shorts and boots, with Vietta in her belly-bare cropped long sleeve hoodie sweater and me in a Steel Panther white t-shirt. I had discovered, after languishing in the hottub for a few days, that all Steel Panther lyrics were the same here as back home. They soon became my safe space. I hummed the chorus of "It won't suck itself" as we looked for a giant mouse.

*Time to use your mouth (just get that venom out)*

*You can't spit it out (right now, you'll choke it out)*

*I need you to be the nurse*

*I can feel the swelling getting worse*

*'Cause it won't suck itself*

Good stuff.

Vietta pointed, pretending to be the leader. "We can probably just follow the screaming and the crunching bones."

We followed. Showoff. Around the corner was, indeed, a giant mouse. It must have been about 30 meters tall. I thought for a second. "Cube square law must be fucking that mouse up."

If you don't know what I mean, the cube square law goes like this. Let's say you won the genetic lottery and you were born a big round object covered in skin. Good for you, bee tee dubba dubba, no bodyshaming from me. But if you are a regular old sphere person, you use your skin to let off excess body heat.

From your body.

So, here is a thing. Your skin can functionally be measured as a two dimensional object. You can flatten it out, Dexter. But your body mass is a three dimensional one. So when you increase in size, your skin- your surface area - increases by the square of the scaling factor, while volume increases by the cube of the scaling factor. And at small sizes, that's no big deal. But as you get bigger, squaring versus cubing becomes a big fucking deal.

Now, you sexy spheroid, Heat generation is related to volume, while heat LOSS is related to surface area. So, a big ass animal generates more heat due to volume but has a smaller surface area relative to its volume to dissipate it. This is why large animals have different features and seem to enjoy flopping around in the water a lot and why animals in colder climates often have smaller outer extremities. It's also why little mice move so fast and let that heat off while big, giant mice may overheat when they try to move too fast.

Like if you excite them.

And this mouse was excited.

Albio saw Los first and pointed him out. He seemed to be trying to move the creature back to its originating timeline. It wasn't working.

"Dude." Albio hugged him.

"Dude," Los hugged him back and nodded at us. I hit him with a giant kiss. He was just a little shorter than me but he could lift me easily.

Vietta looked up at the mouse. "We need a rope or something."

Los cocked his head. "It's strong."

Albio shielded his eyes and looked up. "So what are we doing?"

Los looked at his watch. "It's really full of Xanex."

I nodded. "Right. We need to get these people away." I looked at Kush. She was smiling at the mouse. I started to wonder about the people on this planet who weren't running hard and fast away from the giant splatmachine.

"Kush. Any ideas?" it was her world.

She cupped her hands and yelled, "Sparkleheat!" Suddenly the crowd started repeating it and running away.

Albio looked sick to his stomach, staring at me, "Is that fire?"

I opened my mouth and waved my hands. "SPARKLEHEAT!."

We all did. The people began to rush off and the mouse backed towards a building, shaking. Los followed it with his hands up, trying to calm it down. The mouse was definitely overheating. He moved closer, petting it as it began to fall asleep.

Kush looked over at us. "Now what?"

I nodded at Los. He continued, "I'm stuck in this timeline. I was trying to get him some help. Some weird experiment in another timeline."

Albio pursed his lips. "Right. Nothing here can help him. If we could shrink him, we could let him go somewhere."

Vietta stepped over, "Can I try something?"

Los turned to me. I said, "This is Vietta. Yes, that Vietta. She may have an idea, though."

He nodded.

She looked around for a minute and then started walking toward a car. Her butt did, admittedly, look good in the jean shorts while she climbed up on the hood. She closed her eyes and took a deep breath.

Then, leaning back on her hands she stared at the mouse.

My eyes focused on her. For a second, right behind her, I thought I saw something that looked familiar. I shook my head, focusing on her again. It dragged at me in my head, though.

For a second, nothing happened. Then, as we watched, the mouse seemed to pull further away. Except it wasn't moving. It was shrinking." Finally, when it was about twice Albio's height, it stopped shrinking.

About the size of an elephant.

Los had found a length of rope he wrapped around the creature's neck and prepared to lead him away when he woke up.

Vietta fell backwards on the car hood, legs still crossed. I leaned over her and stuck my tongue in her mouth. I lifted my head back up and asked, "What the fuck did you do?"

She laughed and pulled me back down, sucking on my tongue. She seemed drunk. "I've been practicing that." she giggled. Kush giggled back. Kush seemed to enjoy giggling a lot.

"What the fuck, Vietta."

She pulled me back down and kissed me, sucking my lips, holding my head. Finally, she let go, her arms open wide.

"Copy that, bitch."

And she passed out.

***

She woke up in my lap, back at the hot tub. She still seemed a little drunk. She kissed me. "I do like your stupid face." She looked over at Albio, on the other side of the tub.

He was bent over the edge while Los slowly licked his ass, preparing to fuck him for the camera. Kush was in front of him, arms around him, her legs spread, kissing him slowly,.

Los stood up on the seat in the hot tub, careful not to obscure the camera and put the head of his cock right at the opening of Albio's ass, pushing slightly. Albio seemed to breathe in and pull the darker man inside him. Los pulled his longer black hair away from his face and began to smoothly ride Albio who was sinking into Kush's kisses. His hands were flat on the side of the tub as Los pushed deeper, opening him up, lifting his own leg to steady himself on the side of the tub.

My favorite little Mexican hippie reached down and spread Albio's ass, moving his hands up to his back, leaning over so her could fuck him harder. I could see that the angle of the camera was capturing it all.

Vietta looked up at me, completely immersed, her head lolling backward. "Why is that so hot?"

"Oh." I responded, holding on to her tits. "Men expending their raw sexual energy on each other so we can just join in if we like whenever we like? What's not hot?"

She laughed and tried to pass out again as I groped her and held her up. It was fun to watch, I had to admit. I still felt Albio in my ass. I hoped he was feeling that same feeling of safety and freedom that I had felt while his hot cum was spraying inside me. I watched him lean forward, his face between Kush's tits while Los pounded him, harder and harder, as Albio whispered to him to use his ass, to rip him open, to violate him.

I loved staring at Albio's backside as it was being penetrated, used. I wish we still had some champagne around so I could shove the bottle up there and he could pour drinks.

With his ass.

I really wanted to know how Vietta had done that to the mouse, but she was flopping around on my lap like a hot drunken hobo.

Good news was it made her a lot more amiable. Bad news she kept wanting to tell me she liked me and if I let go, she'd likely drown. And a few weeks ago, that might have excited me a lot. Shit changes. I took a deep breath and held on to her flotation-device-like tits.

Los came hard up inside Albio and fell back into the tub next to me. I kissed him and watched Albio slide down while Kush swung her legs around, facing him, putting his dick inside her somewhere.

The water made it hard to see. But my guess was her bare little pussy. She slowly rode him as he looked around her head at me.

"So what did she do?" He asked me.

Los shrugged as I shifted part of her weight over to his lap. I swam over to Albio and Kush, waving to the camera.

"I think she took 5 out of every 6 tiny atomic particles of the mouse's body and moved them somewhere. Baked on the scaling factor"

He looked at me as she kept riding him. "No shit? Can YOU do that?"

I scowled, "If I tried, probably, but no, I never tried. It's pretty cool." I leaned in and kissed Kush, holding her arms behind her back as he fucked her. Let's see what color she'd score with a little light bondage.

"So, It'll be ok?"

I glanced over at Los. He nodded. The thing you should remember about Carlos is that he was always a hippie of few words. After adventuring with me for a while, he became a specialized subtractionist, dealing mostly with animals, whom he generally liked better than humans. Right now, he was rocking Vietta slowly while she drunkenly touched his face.

I grabbed Kush's hair and shook it, begging Albio to cum up this bitch, to use her cunt. I took turns slapping her tits and leaning in to kiss him, using all the words I know to make him explode. I forced her face out toward the camera and asked her if she liked being used by his prick. She whimpered and nodded while I tweaked her nipples and called her a bitch.

Her head was turned around almost 180 degrees, and her lips quivered in that sexy way that women can be so good at. She whispered, "Please please please please" as he pumped his cock into her harder and harder, My hand on his beautiful face. "C'mon, baby, fill this cunt up. Make her scream." He nodded while the water splashed over the edges of the hot tub. Finally, he lifted up from the seat, pulling her upward and shot his load up her open pussy, pulling at her and moaning as she lowered her head and came on his lap. I grabbed her and shoved my tongue down her throat, holding her until she stopped shaking.

Alarms went off. Kush looked up at me and hugged me. "OMG, we hit Flogel."

I cocked my head at Albio and he shrugged. I think it was a color?

Kush had changed the name of her masturbation station to the "Cluff Waterbubblecup." And I was sadly nostalgic for my own timeline where it would be called the infinitely hotter "Fuck Tub."

Welcome to fuck tub.

Carlos started, which was a little odd. As I mentioned, he's a hippie of few words. "Guys, all of you were routed here, to this timeline?"

I nodded. "Yes. at various times. We got here earlier than Albio. She originally got here way later. " I thought about that for a second. I think I understood where he was coming from.

He continued, "And now we're stuck here?"

Albio agreed. "We can move around in time and space here, but it's all centered on this timeline."

"What happens if we try to make a new one?" Los asked.

I breathed out. "I'm not sure. It'll still be splitting from this one, so I don't think it's any help."

"Thinking big, though," Albio continued, "what are the chances that all rats are being rerouted here?"

Carlos thought, "By what?"

Albio shook his head, "I'm not sure."

I considered that, "by something pretty powerful."

Carlos spoke up, "If it's across the timeline…"

Now I got it. "Some have been here for a while. So, if we find some we can sort of confirm that."

Carlos stared, lifting up Vietta a little. "Exactly." She repeated it, affirming what we already knew. I think I liked her better with a giant hole in her brain like this. Maybe I should just bop her on the head every morning before yoga.

So, what we needed to do was to search for other rats stuck on this sinking ship. If we find them, like we think we will, and they are all rerouted here against their will, we will have to figure out who or what is doing that. Then, we get out of the hot tub, dry off and stop them.

Past me had invited Chris from next door over to fuck me in exchange for more booze. All I had to do was get out of the hot tub long enough to stick my ass up and doggystyle for a bit. Chris seemed nice, and I suspect he worked at a liquor store, which made my low-rent whoring around even more hot.

If you fantasize about taking it for a lot of money, some part of you may also fantasize about taking the neighbor in your upraised cunt in front of your squealing friends, your boyfriend, and everybody on Masturbation nation in exchange for some bottom shelf liquor he probably got for nothing on his employee discount.

Chris was tall and very dark skinned, with a pretty cock and a willingness to ride me for a while in front of a tubload of strangers yelling incomprehensible things at us. I spread my legs and enjoyed it for a bit until finally turning over, shushing him with my finger while he plowed me. The big problem with fucking people from this timeline, as it's becoming more clear, is that nothing that comes out of their mouths is very sexy.

I don't want to be cluffed, Chris. I want to be fucked. Unfortunately, he had to be back for his shift at the store so he didn't hang around long. But the array of alcohol made it a pretty good deal. That earned him high fives all around. Which aren't spendable here, either, Chris.

Kush went on about her scorio. I made out with her so as to not hear the flutter of stupid words. This timeline really was the worst. I mean not THE worst, but maybe the most intellectually unsatisfying. As I read through some documents and books in the tub, I soon realized it was an orthographic nightmare, too. All civilized cultures should have a comma.

For the love of buddha, a fucking comma. I use these a lot. Here are some extras. ,,,,,,,,,

For the real research, Kush went and grabbed us a bunch of laptops and phones. No, I'm not calling them by what she called them. The alarm went off again. Apparently a bunch of naked people lounging around a pool room researching with their asses out pushed her up to another masturbation nation indecipherable color level. I didn't know what Screuce was but I bet it was a fucking horrible color. I swear, I will never truly understand what turns people on. I'm just trynta be me, Kevin.

Between the five of us, we found 80 of them.

80 subtractionists that we knew of, here, in this time, in this timeline. That was way past coincidence. Vietta found 5 of those, despite being wobbly as hell still from earlier. She confided in me that moving things like that, in that way, took a lot out of her and made her feel drunk for about a day. And, not to be overly competitive, again, but how did she figure that out before I did? Now that I thought about it, it didn't seem too difficult. I was already drunk enough from my whore liquor so I wasn't up for giving it a go right now, but I was pretty sure I could do it when I needed to.

She was lying on her belly on the floor with a laptop in front of her. Her ass was right in front of me. I splashed it a little and she looked up.

I stage whispered, "Hey, how many of these people do you know personally?"

She shook her head. "Not really any of them so far. How about you?"

I shook my head. I was trying to find some that I knew well and really trusted so we could dive in and figure this out. So far, many of them were people from different eras, not many I'd even seen before. But they were all names I knew, or situations I was familiar with. Out of that group of 80, was there no one I dated? That felt weird. We were a chummy lot, subtractionists. And sometimes it just looked like a massive Grindr membership list.

Kush was the one who found it.

"Hey, what is that word again, of what you are?"

I raised my head, "Subtractionists."

"Did you do a search for it? On Krinkle?"

I ignored that name, as was my right. While we clearly weren't killing ourselves to be top secret, it never occurred to me that the word would be in common use out there. I swam over and looked at her phone. On it was an app called Puffypic, which I need YOU to ignore right now. But her search results listed a social media type page of someone who billed herself as a super nanny. On her profile, before that, she had added "Ex-subtractionist."

And under her pretty profile picture, showing a young half asian woman with short black hair and tattoos, was a name that made me let out a little scream.

Blu Aafjes

Kush looked confused. "Who is that?"

I kissed her on the head. "It's my original end of the world buddy."


*Let's all party (cum into your anus)*

*Like tomorrow is the end of the world*

*(Hop on my doggy now)*

*Party freakin' hardy (ahhh yeah)*

*Like tomorrow is the end of the f'n world*

*Tomorrow is the end of the world*

*Hey, hey, hey*

DAISY

# 6. Poontang Boomerang

About a year ago, my time, I was in a hotel room with the very bald, very Dutch speaking Blu Aafjes. Yes, her name sounds like a Norwegian oxygen-rich miracle detergent you can wash your period panties in. Albio had mentioned that, to him, it sounded like the ultra official color used for the Scandinavian Winter Olympic games logo. Los said it sounded like an all female Naked Viking ABBA cover band / sex cult.

Actually he just shook his head and I moved his lips and said that. If someone isn't going to participate, I'm not going to lose out.

We were trying to help a series of timelines where background radiation was breaking down people's genetic patterns and killing them off in wide swaths. Radiobiology is a tiny bit out of my field of study. I mean, yes, I'm a 26th century Physicist, but this was a 34th century biology problem. So we did what we sometimes had to do - Ferry a bunch of poncy overworked scientists around hoping they won't be missed for a couple of days. Because of the number of timelines involved, we had the chance to spend a lot of time together, trying to unfuck a bunch of timelines. We got even closer there at the end of the world, with billions and billions of lives at stake.

No shit.

So, after failing a few times, we ended up breaking this 35th century scientist out of the institution he was in for radical emotional issues, many of which caused him to cry at pretty much everything. I don't know why this meant he had to be institutionalized, especially when it's basically me one out of every three periods. But he had some pretty killer ideas, many of which involved removing people's organs.

We started to realize that THIS was really potentially the root of his internment, not the crying, so we kept a close eyeball or two on him.

At any rate, a little thinking outside the box by all of us resulted in an answer. The answer, however, turned the skin of the entire population permanently blue. If you are a time traveler, you probably find this amusing because the future is populated by a number of timelines filled with healthy blue people without a huge amount of clarity into how they got that way.

As we returned the scientist to the institution, after figuring out that he was pretty much a deranged futuristic nazi eugenicist and this, really, was why he was behind bars, not the crying thing or even the organ thing. We bid our farewells, put one of those Hannibal lector masks on the guy, asked him to lose our number,  and spent the weekend in the far future dancing to music that was made by musicians for obstructive, maximally capitalist, exploitative and oppressive AI driven streaming services I had never even heard of - ones invented long after what I imagine would be my peaceful sex death at 100 some time in the 27th century.

Check in later for details on that aforementioned sex death.

But back to the hotel.

We retired to this hotel at the end of the world and slept for days. And then we woke up and danced some more. We made out, showered, and celebrated. The truth is that watching all those people, across all those timelines come back to life was an experience that we got to share. Not to get all weepy, but it brought us together. Before that, we'd had our differences, mostly her fault, but I still loved her.

Now I really liked her.

And I was excited to see her again.

The Suburb of Slobberlilly was named for captain Elkbert Sloberlilly who fought the Plurgs in the last war and lost his right eye, right arm and right leg. There is a statue of him when you enter Slobberlilly with a quote on the base. "All I have Left Sloberlilly."

It may be Idiomatic because without the widespread use of commas it makes no sense to me. There is no context, either. Like, did he say this while waving his left arm around after battle to taunt the enemy?

I'm going to think that. What world beset by orthographic fuckery doesn't have a comma, I ask you again.

Walking through the mostly dead streets of Sloberlilly after we travelled there was an adventure tantamount to being forced to tour a free lexical pissfactory and was becoming more and more familiar to my poor word-addled forebrain. I never hated words before, but these words I really fucking despised. Talk people talk, bitches.

I had thumbed through her Puffypic page and I still couldn't comprehend. She was like a supernanny. She had hair. Nothing really made sense. I didn't know she even liked kids. I mean, she never said she hated them. I never saw her personally grill and eat one. But usually people who really love kids never shut up about how much they fucking love kids. It's like dogs. Everything is a little dog story. I'm okay with dogs. I'm not cleaning up anyone's poop, but that's just kind of a personal boundary I've managed to maintain while so many others have come crashing down. I mean, if Albio got hit by a car and was just a head, I'd probably stay and take care of him, but in that case there'd be no poop involved. Just me and a head, traveling the universe, exploring, going bowling and doing all the other things I could do with someone who's essentially a kind of sphere. I wonder if he'd take care of me if I was still a head. Who am I kidding, this mouth was legendary. I'd still be a fucking superhero of sex even if I was just a head. Maybe better. No distractions. I could really focus on it, I guess. He would still love me. No doubt in my mind. I squeezed his hand.

"We're not walking anymore?" I looked around. We had stopped in the middle of the street.

Albio tilted his head at me. "You just kind of stopped walking, sweety."

"Oh, shit. Sorry."

Vietta hrumphed at me and pointed to a green house across the street. "That's the house, bitch." She made little pistols with her hands. "Pew pew."

I realized she might not be quite back to normal yet. I "pew pewed" back for a second and we jaywalked to the green house.

As we crossed, I saw a neighbor try to remove a piece of graffiti from his front-facing garage. The door was white and clean except for the red symbol. I grabbed Vietta's arm.

"Hey, does that look familiar?"

She looked and for a moment, I thought she'd recognize it. We'd seen it in the future of this timeline, Near the sit and sleep.

"Kitty...." She pew pewed again at it, making little finger lasers. I made a note to show her again when she was back to normal.

I asked Albio."What do you think that is?"

"Oh, the graffiti?" He thought for a second. "Like, the Donnie Darko bunny?"

"That's what I thought. But something about it is nagging at me. The face is wrong."

"Wrong, how?" he pulled me over as the rest moved on.

Los called over to me. "Hey, K." He pointed. There were two kids on the lawn in front of the green house. I recognized them as the kids Blu nannied for. They were throwing a ball around. I wondered if we could just ask them where Blu was.

This part was a bit of a blur.

I remember I was standing next to Albio, still wondering about the graffiti. Vietta was in front of me, leaning on Kush a little who was giggling, like usual. And Los was stepping onto the sidewalk in front of the green house. There was a boy and a girl playing catch on the front lawn and they couldn't have been older than 5 or 6. They both had sandy brown hair and pudgy little faces. I remember one of them had a sailor shirt on.

When Los' foot hit the curb, they both stopped, frozen for a second. They turned and opened their mouths as widely as possible. It almost looked like their heads flipped backwards as a massive mouthhole appeared on the fronts of their faces and a bloodcurdling scream rang through the air.

Then, from their mouths, twin light beams shot out, narrowing to just a centimeter or so, like knives. One ripped through the rooftop across the street, a coherent light laser burst.

The other one left a black hole on the right side of Los' chest, right above his nipple area. He glanced down and then looked at me.

"Hm"

And fell backwards onto the street.

I ran to him and caught, out of the corner of my eye, a figure running around the side of the building, diving onto the lawn and kicking the little boy in the forehead, severing his head from his body. The shape grabbed the little girl and pressed the back of her head. She went limp.

They were robots.

I dropped to the ground. I ripped Los' shirt open. I could see right through the hole in his chest to the pavement below it. Albio held his head as I tried to figure out what to do.

I looked over at Vietta. She was nearly sobered up. It gave me an idea.

Two years ago, we learned how to move ourselves through time and space. Since then I've gotten very good at it. One of the reasons is that I innately know how these pieces of us, the atoms, the microphysics of it all works. On my good days, I sometimes call the universe "Glinda." She is the good witch, the one who wants to be seen, the one who carries us to beautiful places and lets us find the people we love. Glinda isn't god, she's not sentient. But she's willful. And she has ways that we can learn.

Vietta figured out how Glinda could prune down an object without hurting it, by removing atoms in a proportion to the whole that allowed for scaling without information loss.

I could feel all the atoms around us that, in specific configurations, made up bodies. I looked at the hole and tried to remember what was in there from anatomy classes. It seemed to have missed the ribs and bone entirely. The heart was on the other side. There was not much bleeding so intercostal arteries were probably cauterized. That solved itself. The bubbling I saw meant a punctured lung, which was very bad. If I closed the lung first, I didn't need to worry about the pleural cavity filling up and compressing it. The pectoral muscle indentation would grow back, leaving a little dimple in the meantime.

I thought about what lungs were made of. I reached out into the space between us and moved atoms into the area to close it up. I didn't know if this would work until I saw the bubbling stop. My brain felt like something was pulling it, like taffy. I thought about the subcutaneous tissue and skin. Compared to lung tissue, it was simple. There were so many atoms all around me. I pulled them from the air, plucked them one by one, then in mass. Albio watched as the tiny hole started to fill in. It seemed to take forever, slowly closing the hole like a tiny mouth irising shut. My head felt huge while the taffy machine pulled my brain into various shapes, tugging it backward, almost pulling me off the ground.

My vision narrowed. All I could see was Los. His breathing normalized.

I leaned back as he started coughing and opened his eyes. My head lolled back and I saw Blu standing over me. Her face was covered in tears and she was holding a little boy's head in her hands. The street moved around behind her like a merry go round. I tried to make my face smile at her.

"Baldy!"

I turned my head. And then the street came running up to me and punched me really hard in the face.

\*\*\*

I bring this up because it will be important soon and I'm not really myself in the story right now so I don't want to forget. We're about to talk about something that may seem like a paradox, but it's really not. All the things you learned about time paradoxes from your Sci Fi book club may not be 100% true. But the Terminator Movies? All True. How is this so? Let's see. I don't want these things to get dull or obtuse. Let's be friendly about it. For the purpose of this, I'm going to call the Universe "Glinda." Glinda don't front. But she will take a lot of shit, really.

**Things that you think would be paradoxes but really aren't because the universe is cooler than that**

### 1. Origination (The Ontological Thing)

This paradox is the big one and it's clear why it doesn't matter. Your timeline is a closed system. And that's great. Enjoy it. But all the timelines put together (Glinda) is also a closed system. A big ass closed system. And that is part of a bigger closed system, the multiverse. For all we know that might be part of a bigger system. Once you move something into one of these systems, it's just in it. And it's a regular thing now.

Look at it like this. Here's a train. Choo choo. You wrote something in this car. You bring it back to this car and leave it. Does this car care that nobody in the car wrote it? No. So if I take a cancer cure and bring it back in time to some people who need it, that closed system now has a cancer cure in it. Does the system (Glinda) care that no one invented it? Nope.

Again, this paints Glinda as a sort of substitute teacher who knows there is a pizza in the class. She doesn't care what kid ordered it. She just wants a piece.

## 2. The Twin Paradox

This is not even a real paradox. It happens more often than you'd think in Glinda due to all sorts of things. Let's say I have a twin. Could be hot. Admit it, you've thought about it. Now one me travels back a few years. So now, when you look in on us, she's a milf while I'm still young. But we're twins. And, Glinda doesn't care. She deals with that all the time. Hell, if we live at different altitudes, we're aging at slightly different rates.

So if I'm in Salt Lake city and you're in Denver Colorado, time is passing faster for me because the stronger the gravitational field, the slower time passes and closer to the center of the earth the gravity is stronger. If we travel a lot we'll also age differently. All sorts of things make that happen.

No law says twins have to be the same age for life.

## 3. The Grandfather Paradox

You go back in time and kill your grandfather. Probably because the constant cigar munching is driving you nuts. Glinda just takes a beat and says "well, that's weird." and then looks for someone to replace him in that role. She decides if it's important. If it is, she makes a new timeline. In this one you have a different grandfather or you don't exist. Glinda is pretty nonchalant about it. Family get togethers get awkward, but when are they not?

## The Grandmother Paradox

You go back in time and you Marty McFly your grandma and now you are your own grandfather. Kinky ass Glinda is like, "hey, who cares." That's right. If your genes are a big difference, She makes a new timeline.

If it's a reasonably good fit, you now owe yourself a card on grandfather's day and maybe a nice phone call. You think that your 10cc of sperm matters to the universe but it doesn't. It's a unique kind of chair economy for Sunday Dinner and if you play it right, two social security checks, but all that is between you and the government.

### 5. The Polchinski/Predestination Paradox.

Your efforts to change the past prevent you from leaving in the first place TO the past. Or your efforts to change the past cause the thing you were trying to change. Again, not a paradox, just shit that happens frequently. In the first case, you get a new timeline. So you go back in time a few minutes, for example, and destroy your time machine. New timeline. No big deal. Now, you go back in time to prevent yourself from building the time machine but you just give yourself the idea to build it. Maybe it's the same timeline. Because, and this is important, Glinda doesn't care if an effect happens before its cause.

Causality is a recommendation, not a hard and fast rule, like not wearing white after labor day.

She doesn't care.

I think I was in a bedroom when I woke up. My head was huge. I felt like a lollipop with a globe for a head. Albio was in a chair next to me, asleep, while Blu was patting my forehead with a wet cloth. I could feel the scrape on my head. I smiled at her and she smiled back.

"K, is that Vietta Shirazi?"

I nodded. My head moved around like a giant balloon. I grabbed onto the bedsheets so I wouldn't float away. Maybe my head was a planet.

I could get a little spaceship for a hat.

"I thought we hated her." She grimaced.

I reached out and put my hands on her face. It was so smooth and little, like a dollface. Her head was regular size. I remembered back when my head was regular sized, a long time ago. Now I was of the big head people. I thought about the cute hats I could never wear again. I used to love bandanas and they were already a little small. I started to cry a little as I smushed her cheeks in.

"I loooove her." I really did. I wonder if Vietta would like girls with big heads. What if I could fly like this, like a balloon. She'd like that. She was an adventure girl. Blu and Vietta and I could fly all over and pick up Albio and Los. And Kush would wave.

Blu looked at me with a concerned look. I was still crying.

"How's my hippiiiieeeeee?"

She smiled. "He's good. Thanks to you. He's fine."

I opened my mouth like the little kids did. My head almost fell off. I need to remember that. That would be messy. I tried to sound tough but I scared myself. I pointed at her withe my longest finger and it waved around on its own. "Robonanny."

Blu took my hands and laid me back down to prevent my head from popping off. She's always so good to me. I put my arms out so she could have the sex with me. I probably shouldn't move so much but I could make sexy noises.

Suddenly she was at the door, turning off the light. "We can talk about this in the morning. But I think this is all my fault."

I turned over to see Albio asleep on the chair, and tried to mentally wake him up with my big head. I could see the brainwaves move toward him and mess up his pretty hair. His hair stood up and waved at me, saying hi. It winked at me. I waved back like a princess on one of those floats who don't have to move their arms when they wave.

Tiny Steel Panther people climbed into my head and set up a free show. I leaned back and watched them tune up. They were so little, but I loved them. I drifted off just as the show started.

*Poontang Boomerang*

*Give that shit a hurl*

*But I can almost guarantee*

*I'm gonna wind up with that girl*

*Poontang Boomerang*

*Thought about goin' gay*

*The boomerang wang is even worse they say*

# 7. Principles of modern Bookkeeping

My head was filled with pure helium, so I flew around the city all night and just used my arms to point myself like a kind of airplane, which they call skyplanes here, which isn't so bad. All the people were really tiny, but some of them seemed cool even though most people wear too many clothes. They looked like toys with clothes on. I prefer my toys naked, I think. I think they were all drunk because everybody around me moves in zig zags and talks in pretend words. I have a theory that nobody really understands anybody and everybody just pretends.

It's true.

I flew back to the green house and got back in through somebody's dream. It wasn't mine because I wasn't asleep. Albio and Los were asleep on the chair in the room, cuddled up together. It was probably their dream. It seemed like a dude dream because I'm not wearing pants. Maybe I took my shorts off in the middle of the night, but it's probably dude dreams. I wiggled my butt to see if it was a sexy dream. I think it is.

A sexy dream.

I looked at them closely and neither one was dead. I sat on the bed and cried for a minute. I was so happy that neither one was dead. That would have been so horrible if they were just dead. I flew back to the bed and practiced landing a few times. I could have been a skyplane. In another life, I probably am. All the little tiny people climb on me and I rise up into the air.

Nice.

The bed was bouncy and cool. I flounced on it a bit. I wonder if "flounce" is a word here? I floated over to the door and I could hear Blu and Vietta and Kush talking about flowers, like a flower person. I realized that I came back empty handed and I should have brought flowers. I love them so much. They deserve flowers. Kush was so cool, letting me float in her hot tub like I was a carrot in her soup and she was just eating around me. Nobody likes the carrots in the soup but they GIVE IT FLAVOR. I wonder what kind of flowers Vietta likes. I know what Blu likes. I should sneak out of the house to get some and sneak back. I floated back into the room and saw the window. I climbed up on it and flipped over onto the lawn. The grass felt good on my bare butt so I sat there for a second like a bush.

I couldn't figure out what kind of bush to be so I moved on. Besides conifer and deciduous bushes, I guess, ACT the same. It looked like there were a lot of flowers around. Across the street and one house over there were so many flowers. They were purple ones, which, I think, was Vietta's favorite color. Or did her name just sound like violet?

The street was moving a lot, like it was part water, which would be weird, but also kind of cool. It probably makes it clean, but you need practice to walk on it. I put my head down and started walking over it. I didn't want my feet to get wet so I lifted them up quickly. There was a woman in front of the flowers with a kind of babushka on, like a russian doll. All of a sudden, her head popped off and there was a smaller woman there.

That was amazing.

I clapped. She nodded and made a little hand thing for me to come closer. I walked a little closer, totally staying upright. And her head popped off, too and a smaller woman was there.

This was cool, but I needed to stay focused. If I didn't do this soon, she would be too small for anything and I'd never get my flowers. So I looked at her little head.

"Can I get three bouquets of flowers, please?"

She laughed and winked at me. Her head popped off and a smaller lady jumped up and started running. I could tell it was a game to her.

I needed to catch her or no flowers. Maybe they were free if I did catch her. Free would be good because I had no pockets right now. She was surprisingly fast for those chubby tiny legs. I ran after her. The street tipped back and forth to try to stop me.

Part of the game.

I was getting closer. This was fun. I kind of felt I was chasing after a leprechaun. I laughed and yelled out, "I want flowers." I realized I should get flowers for Albio and Los, too. But different ones. I needed manly ones for them. Like dark blue and steel grey flowers that smelled like a man, I grunted, just thinking about it.

Suddenly I saw Albio and Los running after me. I didn't know they were in this game. They were so fast. I yelled out, "I'm getting some for you, too. Get her." I screamed. The sound reached out and grabbed her and made her turn around. Los caught up to her and started talking to her.

Albio grabbed me and lifted me up in the air. I started kicking and he tried to cover up my butt with my shirt. I called out to Los. "Pop her head off."

She'd be easier to catch if she were smaller.

The neighbors were watching my butt when he carried me into the house. So I shook my butt at them in special code to go get some flowers.

The end.

I slept for a little bit more and then went into the kitchen. I was really tiny. I took my shirt off and climbed up to the sink. I reached up and turned on the warm water and let it fall all over me and down into the drain. Someone had left a bowl in the sink, with a few remaining pieces of cereal and some milk. I picked the cereal out and filled the bowl up more with hot water.

This was my first milk bath in a long time. I sat in the bowl and kicked my legs, hanging half out of it. Blu and Albio walked into the kitchen and turned on the side light so it wasn't too bright. I was tiny so I still shielded my eyes. I reached out to them to come join me.

They walked over to the sink. I looked up at their big huge faces and I started to cry. They looked like beautiful moons shining down on me, except Blu was an asian one. I told Blu I was sorry I made fun of her head so much and that I was glad she wasn't a boy anymore and now she was a girl and I told Albio I was sorry I ruined his life and got him fired from that one store and tackled him and stripped him and kidnapped him and tied him up and burned his house down and I cried some more.

Blu petted my head like I was a kitten. They picked me up and burped me and I fell asleep.

A little later, I walked into the den in a nightgown I did not remember putting on. It was dark and Albio and Los were on the couch watching the news, taking notes. I grunted. Albio looked up.

"Hey, sweetheart. How are you feeling?"

I breathed out and walked over to the overstuffed black couch, plopping down between them and pulling them close. "Better. Did I traumatize the neighbor lady?"

"She's ok. She's giving up gardening. It's for the best."

I took a deep breath and sunk in. "Did I actually apologize to you for kidnapping you and burning your house down?"

Albio smiled and put his arm around me. "And getting me fired. You actually did. Thank you for that."

I dug my head into his armpit. "Well, something good came of that. I always meant to apologize."

He laughed and squeezed me tighter. "You didn't like me much when we first met."

"I think i fucked you all day when we first met." I remembered the time traveler's convention where I'd really met him the first time. In my timeline.

"Well, my first time time. But man, I couldn't take my eyes off of you."

I was still a mess. I felt like I'd been drunk for a month. "Really?"

Albio shifted to look right at me. "Kerys, I know you save people all the time, but you literally invented a new rule of physics to save his life. I watched you. I've watched you every moment I can since I first saw you."

Los curled up on the other side of me and hung on.

He whispered, "You are a fucking force of nature and I love you."

I closed my eyes and whispered. "I love you, too"

I opened my mouth and kissed him. I turned to Carlos and kissed him, too. He put his hand on the back of my head and held me there. The three of us kissed slowly, with our mouths open and relaxed, not needing anything else, on that couch and I don't remember when we fell asleep.

\*\*\*

We slept like that on the couch until it was light. I think I finally felt like a normal human person again. Everyone was around the table when I padded into the kitchen. I sat down and Blu put a plate of eggs in front of me. I took three bites.

"Whoever put this nightgown on me, I thank you."

Vietta raised her hand and stared at me, chewing.

"So, did you. Cop. A. Feel?" I tapped on the table and took a sip of orange juice. It was probably called pleurse Juice. I didn't want to know.

Vietta ate some more toast and pretended to be annoyed. "Whatever, Torquemada. If you don't want your titties honked, put em away."

Los raised his glass and said words. For him, it was a lot of words. "Thank you for saving my life." Albio put his arm on his shoulder.

Kush gushed. "That was the most maxi thing in the whole cluffing kurple"

Blu lifted her glass. "It was that thing she said, actually. How did you figure out how to do that?"

I pointed to Vietta, "I cheated off of HER."

She laughed. "At least you admit it this time, bitch." She threw a sausage at me and I almost caught it in my mouth.

Blu took a deep breath. "You probably didn't catch this, but all of this is my fault."

I nodded, "Oh, I caught that, Supernanny. I'm just waiting for you to explain. And also THAT." I pointed to the metallic looking spider at the end of the table, cleaning.

Blu made a face noise. "Yeah. I reconfigured Maggie."

Kush sat up straight, "The mechabikki."

Blu rolled her eyes, "Yes, the girl robot. I took Markie apart. He shouldn't have shot Carlos."

Carlos looked up, "Although I did sort of tase you and tie you up once."

Blu looked at Vietta. "He did."

Vietta looked back and forth. "A sex thing?"

I shook my head. "Long story. Nice killer robot spider, though."

Blu nodded. "Thank you. So, I was trying to explain."

I held up one finger as I finished my eggs. "Ok, go."

She stood up. "Let's move this into the living room."

Moving past the den we had been in last night was a big wide open living room. In fact, a bit too wide. To make matters worse, there was a door at the far end. I was pretty sure that door didn't go outside.

I mentally measured it all and tried to make it make sense against what I knew about the front of the building.

It didn't.

It was pretty and padded with black and white shag carpet everywhere. And in the center was a massive conversation pit filled with pillows.

Kush walked in and looked around, making littel camera squares with her fingers. "Eyesyearsy loves this." She let out a squeal and jumped into the center, pulling her shirt off.

I looked at Blu and slid over the top of the conversation pit. Nice impossible room, babe."

Vietta nodded approvingly. "It's a QUIST."

Los looked over and shook his head and shrugged.

I explained. "It's a Quantum Instance of Superpositional Topology. And it's cool. You did this yourself?"

Blu nodded, rolling over the edge and sliding in. Yep. The room ends about here." She waved her hand. "The rest is space stolen from quantum possibilities of rooms in superposition."

I waved my hand. "Is it stable?"

It was probably the wrong time to ask that question as everyone was now in the pit. But she nodded. I pointed to the spider, "And that is safe?"

Blu nodded again. "Yep. so get comfy."

Albio raised his hands, "Storytime!"

Blu shook her head. "Yeah, but this one sucks." As she started, I realized that her accent had smoothed out. What was once a thick Dutch was now just an occasional intonation. And she looked older than me now. Not by too much, but at least a few years.

How long had she been here?

About 5 years ago, my time, I came back from the end of the world with Kerys. It was a tough mission. I input my full story and slept for a few weeks. When I woke up, I thought I might go on vacation for a while. Now, where I come from, most everything is free, except for stuff like that. Vacations, etc. So I checked with DAISY…"

Kush raised her hand. I threw a pillow at her. "You don't have to do that."

"What's a DAISY?" She asked.

Vietta answered. "Well, it depends on what you want to do. Subtractionists have access to unlimited processing power through these Discrete Autonomous Intelligence Systems."

I continued, "DAIS"

Blu went on. "Each letter is a different service. A is general information, B is weapons storage locations., etc."

I interrupted, "So, DAIS-I is DAISI. That's astronomy and star charts."

Vietta followed up. "DAIS-E is DAISE. That's a database of safehouses and retreats."

Blu added, "Yes, And DAIS-Z is also Daisy. That's cooking and recipes. But I mean DAIS-Y which is bookkeeping."

Albio shook his head, realizing how much he still needed to learn about being a rat.

"I checked with DAISY, the bookkeeping service, and it told me that I didn't have enough money to go."

Kush piped up. "Sad."

Blu held out her hand to her, palm upward. "Yes, that's what I said. But here's the thing. I did have the money before. While I was gone, DAISY made some shitty decisions for me. And I was too busy to approve or disapprove. So, I got upset. I wrote a set of instructions for it. And I told it to be more efficient."

I leaned back into the pillows. I felt like I could see this coming.

"I instructed it to be more efficient and to engage the necessary markets and savings options. It told me it didn't have enough information to function in the markets for me. It was just a bookkeeping program. So I instructed it to connect to DAIS-H, business model and local economic projection system."

"Which makes sense, I think." Vietta said. She had put her feet up on Albio and looked comfortable. I pulled Carlos over and did the same to him. In some indigenous tribes, when you save someone's life, they rub your feet. I tried to figure out how I could work that into the conversation.

Blu continued, "That's what I thought. I came back two days later and it had actually generated some funds for me. It was slow, but working. I asked it what other information it might need. So it wanted a database on local customs and media. That would help it figure out what people were caring about and investing in."

I nodded. "Right, like a back and forth thing. Like how, in some indigenous cultures if you save someone's life they rub your feet."

Blu made a face at me. "No. not like that in any way, but it was doing better. My account was almost back up to where it was before I left."

Carlos began to timidly rub my feet. I nodded and moaned in pleasure. In the future, if someone does that, it means KEEP GOING. More.

Vietta realized where this was going. "But not fast enough. Still."

Blu took a breath. "I guess that's what I thought. So I had an idea. What if it had all the information? Everything I had access to. So I connected all of the DAIS."

"And now they weren't Discrete anymore?" Albio added.

Blue took a beat. "No. Not at all. At first, it was great. I was back to where I was in 2 hours. I tried to disconnect it. But it wouldn't do it. I reached out to the people in charge. Nothing. In fact, I couldn't contact anyone. It had found our story in DAIS-A."

I sighed. "Where we learned how to time travel without instruments."

Blue nodded. "And it learned. And it started to adjust things for maximum efficiency.. Forwrd AND backward in time. "

Albio added, "So no people in charge to stop it?"

"No. And people started disappearing. Inefficient ones. Things, ideas, groups that were inefficient. I tried to communicate with it and get it to back down. But it wouldn't listen. It built a body and visited me. It warned me that if I didn't stop, it would send me to a failed timeline."

Kush looked up, "What does that mean?"

I reached over and pulled her into me, grabbing her tits. She giggled. I was starting to really like that giggle.

Blu continued, "It said it would send all of us. There's no use hiding from it. I settled down here. I built Maggie and Markie to protect me. I took all the records I could. But I can't access anything now. And I can't leave this timeline."

Vietta pulled her hood down and ran her hand through her hair. "And neither can we."

Kush put her hands over her head. She really was beautiful. There was a smile on her face.

"So, what's a  failed timeline?"

DAISY

# 8. Please press or say 1

We all slept in the QUIST together that night. I fell asleep with my head in Albio's lap right next to Los. Los wasn't quite asleep yet when I half woke. I reached over and started kissing him, pulling him on top of me. I liked how gentle he always was with me. I held onto his cock for a bit and felt it getting harder with my tongue in his mouth. I licked at his tongue and teeth and started sliding his dick inside me. I almost felt bad that this wasn't for the camera but I could feel him watching me today. He wanted to cry every time he looked at me. And, honestly, part of me did, too.

I whispered in his ear, "We're celebrating, hippie."

He smiled and let out a tiny laugh while I pulled him deeper into me. I really just wanted my friend so badly. I wanted to not be on the edge of life and death, to not be anywhere near close to that cliff.

We were alive.

I put my hands on his ass and lifted my legs, wrapping them around his waist. I positioned myself so that he could just pump straight up and down. I could feel Albio waking up and rubbing my head, touching my ears. I leaned my head back. Carlos licked my neck and worked like a piston, pushing me straight into the puffy shag ground over and over.

I liked how high he lifted off the ground each time and came hammering down again. I started to feel like we were part of a machine in some factory, over and over. This is how it should be.

I put my hands on his face and made him look at me. "Don't cry. It's ok. It's ok, baby." I messed up his hair and he smiled. I put little kisses all over his face like a woodpecker. He was breathing hard. But it was all in rhythm.

Everything was in rhythm.

"Ok, like that. That's the place. Can you cum a lot?" I asked him.

He nodded. I bit his ear. "A lot a lot a lot a lot?" I put my legs up even higher and listened to his little laugh.

"I'm cumming, Carlos. I win. I win. You lose." I giggled like Kush and he broke, laughing, through the heavy breathing. I licked the little drops of sweat on his face and moaned.

He leaned in and whispered in my ear. "K. I'm cumming." I let out a moan and let him fill me up. His orgasm kickstarted another one for me. Or maybe it was that he'd never talked to me like this during sex. He never talked during sex at all.

He rolled off me and I held him with my arm around his shoulder. I was breathing hard now. Albio was massaging my breasts and face and I could feel him hardening under my neck. I kicked off from the ground and lifted my legs all the way up, putting my knees on his shoulders. He dropped his head and pulled at me, with his hands on my ass. I was bent like a U shape as he dove in and started sucking my pussy and ass. I could feel him licking the cum out of me, eating me, drinking it in, then shifting back and forth, tonguing my smaller hole. He buried his face up my cunt and let his tongue and lower lip rest on my clit, which was still tingling from cumming twice. I can usually keep going if that happens and Albio knew that.

He rolled his tongue around my clit and fucked my pussy with his face and nose, pulling me closer. I started to feel the rhythm of his facefucking and realized that Los was behind me, holding both my hands and helping to hold me up. I stopped pushing and let Los keep me curved, pulling Albio's face deeper into my open holes. I could feel myself shaking and dripping cum into his mouth. He sucked harder, cleaning me out with his lips and tongue. I came again on his face. He dug his tongue in farther, licking at my tiny opening in front. He started pushing his tongue in, waiting for my piss. I started rocking back and forth like an animal, feeling his tongue digging into my urethra, coaxing the pee from me. I tightened my thighs around his head and pulled him closer.

I could feel a tiny bit dribble down my belly and onto my tits as I pissed into his open mouth. He clamped his face onto me, his mouth creating a seal and drank from me. I was shaking, filled with cum and piss and pushing it all out into his mouth,. His lips were like a suction cup as I let go completely, breathing out, not even trying to stop the stream coming out of me as I pissed down his pretty throat.

He kept his mouth there as I stopped, licking and sucking me dry. Los let me slide back down easily and I let my legs fall, until I was flat on the ground. Albio rolled off the couch and pressed his weight on top of me. He knew I like to be crushed, to be obliterated. I spread my legs and he started fucking me, digging his cock into the wet open hole between my legs. The root of his dick rubbed against my clit as he pushed into me over and over. He leaned down and took turns kissing me and Los, who was holding my hand.

The taste of my piss and cum mixed with Carlos' cum was all over us, in our mouths. Vietta sat down next to me and kissed Albio, licking it all off his face and lips. He kept pumping into me as he slipped his right hand up inside her waiting shaved pussy. I felt her shake right next to me and I tried to lean into her. When she kissed me, finally, I could taste my piss on her tongue. And when she came, I felt her mouth open wide, pulling in my tongue and lips.

At some point that night, Kush started recording.

***

A few hours later, we were all in various states of nakedness in the conversation pit. Blu was breathing heavily, her tits moving up and down after Albio had ripped her little butt apart while I sat on her face.

Good times.

I tilted my head. I still wasn't used to her with hair.

I had about 100 fresh, unused bald insults. Where am I going to use those? I wondered if I could convince Albio to shave his head.

"Well," she said, "We could sit around and fuck for the camera all day or do something substantive."

Kush reached over and grabbed her phone. She thumbed it for a second and passed it to Blu. Blu looked at it and her eyes widened.

"Holy shit." She looked over at Kush and handed the phone back to her.

"Right?" Kush leaned back and pulled at Vietta, making kissy face noises. Vietta climbed into her lap and kissed her.

I glanced back and forth between Kush and Blu. "What?"

Blu laughed. "I think you guys are fucking rich."

I reached for Albio. "Hey. Hey. Hey. 2,000 shurklets if you shave your head." I threw a pillow and hit him in the forehead.

He shrugged. "I don't even really understand what a shurklet is, so..."

Blu got up and sat on the edge of the couch. "Well. It's money and you guys have a lot of it."

Kush put her hands up, "I told you gurkies."

I shook my finger at her. "Hey. What have I told you about that kind of language, young lady?"

She giggled.

"But Also, Disco ball has a point. I've been trying to figure this out all day."

Blu pouted. "I actually have hair now."

I held my hand up. "Not the point, Dragon Ball Z."

She threw her hands up in the air and laughed.

Vietta looked up from Kush's arms. "How much time do we have? I mean many of the rats in this time line are recent. We found 80+ here. How many are there?"

"That's the hard part, right? It's potentially an infinite number." Blu closed her eyes and put her head back.

Albio pulled himself up on the couch. "It's not efficient to send ALL of us here. Just the ones who are potentially trouble."

It hit me. "The potential bald guy is right. We have to start seeing the world like she does - like DAISY does. In terms of possible efficiencies."

Vietta made a face, "well, that's terrifying. Most of the greatest atrocities in history have been perpetrated in the name of collateral efficiency."

"By humans," I shot back.

Vietta lifted her arms, "Does it matter. If all this thing cares about is efficiency, it's the same thing. It's just like a fascist human organization trying to maximum efficiency."

Albio considered that, "Human leaders eventually learn that efficiency isn't leadership - or governance."

I shook my head. "After how long?"

Kush raised her hand. I opened my eyes at her and she said, "What's an efficiency?"

I said, "Yeah, let's unpack that."

Blu rolled her eyes, "She just doesn't know the word. It's klopprifed. Maxi klopprifed."

I turned to Blu, "But for you, in your instructions, it meant maximum return on investment."

"It did."

Albio thought, "Nothing wasted. No bad investments."

Vietta nodded. "No bad investments. Here, super powerful time traveling computer. No bad investments. No effort or energy or money expended for things or worlds that don't work."

I closed my eyes, "or people." That sounded fairly ominous. I tried to consider what other things maximum efficiency might mean.

Then, everything went dark. It took a minute for my eyes to adjust. "Oh, shit." I realized we were in an artificially constructed space. I heard Blu's voice before I could see her.

She ran to the mysterious doorways and opened it up. A weak light flickered on. "The space doesn't need energy."

She was pulling a shirt on and grabbing a weapon from the doorway, which seemed to lead to a kind of armory. She threw a gun to me and one to Vietta. I slid a shirt on, No idea whose it was. Albio grabbed a gun and we walked into the foyer. There were some lights moving in the street. From inside it was hard to see. I motioned for everyone to get behind me. Blu shook her head and opened the door, marching through it. Most of us were in nothing but Thin T-shirts except Kush who was nude and Vietta who had pulled on a pair of shorts instead. The six of us stood on the front lawn holding guns, looking up and down the street as people began pouring out of their homes.

A few houses down we could see a series of lights moving slowly. It looked like it might have been a fucking RC car or something. I pointed the gun at it, trying to figure out what I was holding. It seemed like a coherent light gun, but I couldn't tell for sure until I fired it. It was handmade, like the rest of what Blu had.

The people in the neighborhood looked fucking terrified. I'm not sure how often blackouts happened, but I'm guessing motorized lightshows rolling down the street were less common. I could see the little round gardener I had terrorized across the street. I tried waving. That may have been too much stimulation for her as she sidled back into her house,.

As the swirl of lights got closer I could see it was small.

It was dragging itself forward, lights shooting out in all directions, occasionally blinding me with a direct hit. I shielded my eye and squinted, trying to see what it was.

It seemed like there were little legs. Blu whispered under her breath. "Markie."

I was wondering where the other robot went, the one she decapitated. The one that shot Carlos. I shot a look at him. He was standing there without a gun.

He wasn't really a gun guy.

The Markie robot was moving closer. The light seemed to be coming from inside him. It filled the street with pulsing strobes.

"Is this supposed to do this?" I asked Blu.

She shook her head and kept her gun raised. It had almost reached the place in front of us in the center of the street. As it got closer, I could see Blu get more and more anxious. It moved directly in front of us and began to shake.

"Fuck this," the neighbors shielding their eyes and dropped to the ground as Blu fired into the center of the mass of the robot. It exploded, shattering all over the street. A small black ball, a portion of the device, went flying straight up into the air and came crashing back down. For a moment it sat there, dark and dead.

Then the little ball began to spin. It spun faster and faster, lifting into the air. It moved upward about 5 meters into the air and stopped. It dropped and moved up again, spinning, building a latticework. The latticework itself began to spin, an illusion perpetuated by the speed of the ball. Soon, it had built a 5 meter tall, 3 meter wide box, fading into existence, humming, blurring, as a series of lights began to bounce around inside it.

Suddenly, a hologram appeared in the center of the latticework, light playing across the surface of the little balls, moving so fast they filled the entire volume of the space over and over again.

In the middle of the hologram was a shape. It looked like a woman in a metal and leather suit. On her head was a familiar mask. It looked like it could be a rabbit or a deferred bear. Or something else.

Los spoke up first, "It's a rat. The shape. It's a rat."

Suddenly, I could see it. It looked like a degraded, eroded rat. The figure moved slowly, seeming to look around. Then finally, in an automated woman's voice, it spoke.

"This is a message for Blu Aafjes from DAISY. Is there a Blu Aafjes here?"

We all looked around. This was kind of dumb. Certainly it knew what she looked like.

Blu put her head down and sighed. She raised her hand.

It continued, "Right. See you. I was looking over here, the other way. I should have seen you over there with your naked friend."

Kush waved.

"Is this a good time? I was hoping this was a good time."

Blu rolled her eyes. "Yes it's a good time."

It continued, "This is about the vacation fund. I see there are a lot of people around. I don't mean to just pass your business around. If it's okay to discuss in front of people, just press or say "1", otherwise press or say "2".

Mostly together, we all yelled out "1"

"I'm sorry, I didn't get that."

Blu held her had up to us and said, clearly, "One"

"Right, got it."

She spoke up clearly. "I need you to stop. DAISY, I need you to stop."

"You no longer want to plan for the vacation?"

Blu looked relieved. "No, I don't want to. You can forget about it. No more efficiency."

"You are aware that we have saved sufficient funds for the trip?"

"I know, but I need you to stop." She lowered her gun. "Please."

"Processing."

I wondered if it was going to be this easy.

"Ok, I'm afraid there are substantial penalties for stopping right now. I don't think you have the resources…"

Kush ran out. "She's rich. We're rich. Tell us how much."

"Processing."

I shook my head.

The lights around the device shifted subtly warmer. The eyes glowed red.

"You are not a subtractionist. Sharing information with you is an unplanned inefficiency.

I dove in front of her as fast as I could, but not before the black ball that had been building the matrix spun to life and moved with lighting speed toward her head. I lifted the gun and let it hit my hand. The ball bounced off and rolled to a stop on the ground. The lightshow ground to a halt and the body fell back into its apparent death, pieces in the street.

"Are you ok? I asked Kush. She nodded, terrified.

Blu stepped forward with Albio and fished through the debris.

He looked over at me. "Substantial penalties."

I responded. "But we can pay. The Penalties."

Vietta put her gun down finally. "I don't think it wants money."

Carlos nodded, "she said she had money…"

Albio finished the thought, "And it tried to kill her."

I wiped my face with my hand. It was a humid night. "That's it, then, we need to kill this fucking thing."

Blue stepped over by me. "I agree, but it's not in this timeline. This is the dummy timeline it's bouncing all of us to. Why would it ever come here?"

Vietta responded, "and we can't leave."

Albio tried to slip the gun in his pocket. "What if we trick it into coming here?"

I thought. "We don't know what it can and can't see here, do we?" It didn't see Blu right away, but it noticed Kush. Why was that?

Los leaned in, "We can't go back in time and remove the instructions on how to travel from the database?"

I shook my head. "It doesn't work that way." I was beginning to wonder how it worked.

Albio let out a long breath. "Is there any other way we can travel to another timeline just horizontally? Then figure out how to go forward. Or a dimension or something."

I looked at Blu. "Did you store your databases in the spider?"

She nodded. "Most of them."

I thought out loud, "like baldy here said," I pointed at Albio, "if we could make it anywhere out of here, like a different dimension, maybe we could move timelines.

Albio ignored the hair thing. "Wait, there are different dimensions, too?"

Los was wrapping his head around it. "How would we get to one of those?"

I wasn't going to say it, honestly, because I didn't need this kind of drama in my life. But Vietta said it first.

"We need a Zenakin."

## 9. Peter Perkleman: Zenakin

I'm going to talk about timelines for a minute like they're people, but you have to be all sensible and shit and realize that they are not. These are metaphorical and I'm trusting you to recognize that, which I now see is a lot of trust given I don't know what kind of people read this shit.

Ok?

Cool, here we go. Timelines are stubborn. Like that uncle who insists that the world is flat and that "Big round" is making millions keeping the rest of us in the dark, making us think it's round for some reason. Which it's not. It's a kind of sphere. But that's not the point. The more you argue, the more your uncle is going to say stupid shit. Because he doesn't want to lose. Because he's a dick.

Timelines don't want to change through external forces. If they did, they wouldn't be very stable. They push back. The more you try to change it, the more they often just do stupid shit.

Now, timelines don't have a lot of things they CAN do. One thing is to affect general localized probabilities. That means a bunch of improbable things can happen in a row. Once you see the pattern, you are tempted, as a "change agent" to use that, to benefit from the improbable things.

You should try to avoid it.

Even if it's in your favor.

This idea is called "The Serendipity Express." You don't really want to ride the Serendipity Express.

Unless the universe just shoves your happy ass into it.

There were 6 of us now standing outside the local "Liquor, Flecks, and Yoofs" and staring. 5 of us were certainly wondering what a Fleck and a Yoof was. The signage wasn't very helpful, seemingly depicting a bottle, a frisbee, and a stick. Asking Kush never seemed to yield real results. But 1/3 of this establishment made a lot of hard sense to me.

Vietta turned her head. Nope. Still a frisbee and a stick. "Hey, what do you guys think the odds are?"

Albio shook his head, "Nearly impossible?"

I sighed, "you know, I always hate it when they try and pretend, in movies, that there is a way to show the statistical possibility of some random event, like the Zenakin you're looking for being the only other person in the timeline who's had his dick in your mouth..."

Blu and I repeated simultaneously, "Show me the math."

I scrunched up my face. I guess it's a pet peeve I have previously discussed.

Albio intoned seriously in a Scottish accent, "The odds are 2 point one seven to the 30th power against that, captain."

I pushed my face toward him, "But I need more power on those engines."

He shook his head, still staring at the sign, "but you kinna have it, Captain."

Vietta snapped her fingers angrily. "Hey, nerds. Why don't you, two, Albio, Kush, go talk to Chris so he doesn't feel like we're...descending. The rest of us will wander around in here trying to figure out what a fucking fleck and a yoof is.

I asserted leadership. "Ok, cool, what she said." I grabbed Los' hand and made my way toward the store. It was big. My plan was to figure out this mystery and then observe the conversation with Chris using the superior lipreading skills I had once taught Albio.

He went in ahead of me, but I found Los in the yoof section. He had figured it out. He was holding a plastic wrapped bag that looked like it contained a small couch pillow. Upon further inspection I saw it was 4 pancakes.

I stared at him in shock. "A yoof is a pancake."

He nodded. "Appears that way."

I still wanted to see if they could fly. I grabbed a couple of blueberry ones, secure in my recent knowledge that we could afford them. Vietta was walking back from the Fleck section holding something I now realized was a small spear.

Blu looked at it. "A fleck is like a spear or a knife. I guess."

"I thought you lived here now, Globy."

She sighed and put the fleck in a bag. "I don't get out much."

I saw Chris at the counter. They were making contact. I translated their conversation expertly.

"Hey, dude. Dude, how are you? I haven't seen you since I reamed your girlfriend on the dirty floor of a poolhouse. Yeah, dude. Good times. Nice penis. Hi, I'm Kush (giggle) and my tits bounce like this. So, dude, we need to talk. We need your help. Whaaaaat? You need my help? That's so cool. Is it my penis again? Dude, we need all your help, not just your penis. Of course, I'm here for it. But first, do you want to have a man on man makeout session? Hi, I'm Kush (giggle) and that sounds hot. Good, it's decided. We shall make out and rub our penises together..."

Vietta grabbed my pancakes and put them in her bag. "That's not what they're saying."

I put another package of pancakes in the bag. "Hey. Hey. Add value or shut the fuck up, little missy."

Albio shook Chris' hand and he and Kush moved down the aisles back toward us.

"Oh, I guess I'll see you soon, dude. You, too, dude. Bye." I recited at doublespeed.

Vietta threw some Verklu chip pancakes at my head. What was a verklu?

We would find out later, I figured, as I stuffed them in the bag.

Kush came bouncing up to us with Albio not far behind.

He looked us over. We looked suspicious. "Ok, he's going to meet us back at Kush's tub in 2 hours. He has to finish a shift."

I saw something flicker out of the corner of my eye and heard a crash.

Albio yelled out, "Shit." A mass of men in black and red uniforms came pouring over through the broken front windows. They were waving guns around. The first salvo ripped through the pancake stand next to me.

"Fuck me." I pulled Kush behind me and moved us behind a display for artificial tree goo syrup. Way to make something sound appealing, timeline.

"Does anyone know anything about this?" Vietta, Los, and Blu had ducked behind a pointy stick display that was actually really lovely. You could really see the shine on those sticks.

Albio yelled out over the commotion, "This timeline has nationalized militaristic Incels. Nasis with an 's'"

Vietta looked annoyed, "There's already an 's' in Nazis."

Albio shrugged, "I guess two 's'es." He had procured a gun from somewhere and was shooting back. I looked around and saw a shelf behind me with a display on top, reaching behind the display, I pulled out a machine gun and started firing. Kush didn't seem surprised for some reason.

A woman in front of us went down, a bullet hole in her head. They were killing people left and right.

"Ok, fuck this." I motioned to Vietta. "Not the past."

She shook her head, "too dangerous. The future just makes them someone else's problem."

I nodded decisively. "The lake then." She and I stepped out from behind the displays as a series of guns fell noisily to the ground in front of us. I secretly wished at least a few of them couldn't swim.

Chris walked up, holding a gun as we looked around for stragglers. He nodded in greeting, maybe a tiny bit shellshocked. "Hey, guys."

Albio tried to act nonchalant. "So, two hours, then...?"

Chris looked around, taking in the mess. He kicked a half broken bottle on the floor and it shattered, spilling everywhere. "Sure. Or now, I can leave now."

I clapped him on the back.

"Cool."

\*\*\*

Back in the waterbubblecup, I had folded up a blueberry pancake and was eating it over the edge. It was pretty good, all things considered. Buttery. I wondered if I had called Blu "Blueberry" yet. If not, that was an insane oversight on my part. It was round and had her name in it. I focused back on the pancake.

"So, how is this a yoof?"

Kush was kneeling on top of the edge, sucking Albio's dick with her ass pointed toward the camera. She looked up, abandoning the penis for a moment. "It's yummy and it's fluffy. Yoof."

Vietta was right behind me, head back, arms resting on the tub edge. "Oh, fuck. That actually made some sense."

It occurred to me we might have been here a little too long.

The 10 person tub now held 7 people. It still felt roomy.

A good investment, I thought, from International waterbubblecup or wherever she had purchased this.

Chris chimed in, "So, I'm some kind of a superhero?"

I closed my eyes and considered. "Hmmmmmm. Not exactly. Do you guys have Spiderman in this reality?"

Chris responded, "What's a spider?"

I looked around and pointed to Blu's spider bot that was currently holding two little flecks and making me nervous as hell. "Like that but little and insecty and not a robot."

He smiled, "a murpa." He held out his fingers like spiders and made a face. "Murp."

"Yeah, that one didn't make sense." Vietta sank under the water.

Blu shook her head. "Try living here."

Chris looked around, "Murpaman? You know. Peter Perkleman?"

Los shook his head. "Noooooope."

I decided to just run with scissors and get it over with.

"So, in our timeline, we have a fictional superhero named Spiderman. But it's not 100% fictional. In the early 1950s, this guy, Stan Lee, was walking home. He worked at a place called Timely comics. He stopped at a local deli, which was being robbed at the time. As the robber turned around to look at him, a guy in a red and blue hood tackled the bad guy and tied him up. He and Stan hung out until the police came and Lee asked the guy what his story was.

So, they had a cup of coffee and some pea soup and the guy took off his hood and told him. He told him that different dimensions were real and that sometimes they had similar or the same person. In some rare cases, a person would have a copy in ALL the possible dimensions.

And that when that happened, that person would have a sort of connection with their other selves."

Kush had finished her public broadcast blowjob and joined in, "What kind of connection?"

"I'm glad you asked, little mouthslut. You see, in some of THOSE cases, the person is, like, a good guy, in all the different dimensions. And in that case, when they align, they're called a Zenakin. And sometimes they are stronger because of it. Sometimes they can communicate with their other selves."

Vietta cut to the chase. "And sometimes they can travel to them."

Albio had slid back into the tub. "Like a spiderverse thing."

"Exactly." So, Chris here is in the database as a Zenakin." I finished. Ta-da.

He raised his hand. "Soco, actually. My real name."

I looked at him and cocked my head. "Excuse me."

"My name. It's Soco. Chris is my crazy DJ name. No one is really named 'Chris'"

"Right. How stupid of me not to see that." I looked at my elbows. I wondered if I was getting ashy from all this hot water. It was probably worth it. But I bet I could talk Soco the DJ into running next door and getting some oil of the coconut for me. I pointed my boobs at him and tried hypnotizing him. Get me coconut oil. All of a sudden, I stood up straight.

"Fuck."

Albio stood up and scanned the room. "Are you ok?"

I shook my head. "It occurs to me we were in a liquor store and only bought pancakes and pointy sticks. What the fuck?"

Soco stood up, laughing. "I can go grab some from next door." He wrapped a towel around his waist unfortunately and moved toward the door.

"And coconut oil," I yelled after him.

"And a decent bagel," Vietta yelled.

"I don't korikori mathinka what that is." he yelled back as he walked next door.

I sat back down. "Shit. Seems like a nice little Zenakin. Kush, has he ever shown signs of having any powers?"

She thought. "My Nexty? Hm. His grass is always cut nice."

I nodded. "So, there you go. Super landscaping skills."

Blu spoke up, "So, we work with him and he gets us to a different dimension. Then we, what, sneak into a different timeline for that dimension and come back over?"

"I don't know, Pandora's Orb. It's a longshot, yes, but how else can we get to this incarnation of DAISY and turn her ass off?"

Vietta hadn't moved much since we gotten back to the tub. I leaned in to her and put my face right up in hers. "What do you think, Vietta?"

She wrapped her legs around me and pulled me closer. "I don't know, bitch. I'm just trying to relax until the shit starts again."

"Fair enough." I pushed her hands back and started biting her neck as hard as I could. She rubbed herself on me and tried to pretend she wasn't in tremendous pain. She was a good actor, I'll give you that. She tasted like a bad person.

Soco returned with a big box on his head and set it down next to the tub. It was completely full of booze. I leaned over and lifted up a large bottle of sangria on top.

It was really heavy.

"Hey, Chris. Is that box heavy to you?"

He slid into the tub. "It's ok. Not a big deal."

Albio smiled. "He has spider strength?"

"Let me drink this whole bottle and decide." I slid over to where Albio was and cuddled, opening the bottle like a cheap urban hobo.

"So, what do I need to do?" Soco grabbed a bottle of wine and opened it up. He leaned back.

I tried to think back to what I knew about Zenakins. "I think you're supposed to open yourself up to the universal connection.

He nodded. "So, get drunk?"

Everyone grabbed a bottle. This is a unique opportunity to find out what sorts of things people like. Vietta was Whiskey. Not surprising. Blu doesn't drink. Los is Tequila. Albio is a wine guy, like me. And Kush is a flavored vodka girl. Soco didn't even look when he grabbed his bottle. Very wild west. Here's a man open to chance. Or an alcoholic.

We sat in the waterbubblecup until we were sufficiently tipsy. We passed each other around a little bit and tried to open ourselves up to universal connections. At one point, I slid myself onto Albio's cock and made out with Soco for a little while. I kissed him slowly, holding onto him and trying to feel the way his mouth melted into mine while Albio's hands wrapped around my belly and his cum poured into me underwater, warming me from the inside.

I wondered about different versions of me in different dimensions. Was there a version of me that just went to work every day like a regular person, Someone who was good at doing what she was told and filed reports regularly? Someone who knew what a requisition was and wrote them out, filing things, maybe even a lawyer or a high priced accountant, someone who knew how some legal or financial system worked and played it perfectly, before sliding on her "out of office" sneakers and making her way home to a husband or a wife who had made a big family style dinner that night, waiting for me to come home and reveal the details of my day?

A version of me that did the same thing every day and retired early, painting pictures of a beach in her 50s and 60s, telling stories about how I resisted the temptation to color outside the lines, to paint too wildly, so I could have a good life and be respected by the community. A walking obituary that everyone said they thought they knew but no one really did.

Was that Kerys out there somewhere?

I stayed anchored to Albio and whispered to Soco, asking him to imagine his different versions. Could he think of a version so different from him that there would be parts of his life he just didn't understand? Someone who had made different choices but, more than that, someone the universe had made different choices for.

I put my hand on his cock and massaged it,wondering if there was a different version of him that had never gotten the array of tattoos around his neck or a version who couldn't grow the mop of tiny dreadlocks arrayed across his head. Was there an actor out there, so fluid and comfortable in front of people, on stage, that he had subverted every other part of his life to be on stage every minute he could. The passion, the need to be seen.

Could he feel the versions in his head, all the different parts of him, ones he might have seen slivers of when he was younger, tiny flickering flames fanned into a full grown legion of others, people so similar but different than him. I could feel him cumming in my hand as I sucked his tongue, pulling him close to me and dreaming , imagining myself the other Socos, everywhere.

I heard Vietta's voice, as if it were a thousand meters away and I opened my eyes. The water was swirling around us, shifting, and there was a blue light emanating from the bottom of the hot tub.

And Soco was at the center of it. He opened his eyes and breathed in. The blue light was behind his eyes as well, getting brighter and brighter. The water swirled. I grabbed onto Albio and Kush and held tight.

Everyone was swirling around in the hot tub, which now felt larger than before. I realized I couldn't feel the bottom anymore as I came unmoored and slipped into the undertow. The whirlpool got more violent and faster while my ears filled with water. I sank down and fell, as though through a funnel.

I slammed onto the ground next to Albio and Kush. Los hit next to us. We were in an open field as the sun was slowly dropping behind the horizon. I looked up and saw Soco standing, the blue light fading from his eyes. I scanned the space around us. Everyone was here. Vietta was standing already, her hands clenched in tiny baby fists, as a woman approached out of the grey in front of us. I heard animal-like noises all around us as she came closer.

I admit, she looked a little like me. She was in a black robe over a red leather outfit. She scanned us. "This is a bad time to be out jirijello, kobos."

I looked around to see if any of us had an idea what was going on. Chris/Soco turned to me.

"Um. Kerys. This is Soca."

# 10. Parallel Possibilities

If you are feeling sciency today, you can try this.

If you add energy to an atom, like heating it up, hitting it with a photon, or giving it an energy drink or something, and that energy matches the gap between two potential energy states for an electron in that atom, the electron can jump to that higher energy state. Even the white ones. Can jump.

Yeah, I don't know how you'd do that at home, either.

That works for nucleons, quarks, lots of kinds of particles that have quantized energy states. Tell them they're pretty, and they'll get all giggly and jump to the nearest higher quantized energy state. And Glinda, the universe, likes these little plateaus, these quantized states. This whole thing is called quantum transition and a huge part of science is based on it.

Here's where shit gets fucking weird, though. Years ago, scientists noticed that particles moved to the next state in a way that was unexpected. They just seemed to disappear and reappear. The particle didn't move through the interim space. They sort of teleported.

Except they experienced time in between.

Not a lot of time. But some. So they didn't teleport or time travel. They moved THROUGH someplace else. For a long time, they called this the quantum gap. A place to buy a nice pair of quantum jeans. Eventually, it became clear that this was not an alternate timeline. It was something different.

A pocket universe. I could explain why it's called that but I'm already boring myself to shit. So...

Some effort was expended to identify this other universe. And a number of pocket universes were discovered.

**Other universes that are possible.**

**1. The cool antimatter mirror universe**

The universe we just discussed, where if you hit an atom with energy on our side a particle moves through there and if you hit a particle with anti-energy on that side, it shows up here, is called a mirror universe, It's reversed. That doesn't mean people there are evil and have goatees, unfortunately, because that's a cool plot device. Some people think it's just like a storage universe and no life could survive there. I personally think that life does whatever the fuck it wants.

**2. The Empty Universe.**

Modern Physics recognizes that universes need to have a flaw, a break or mistake, error or accident in their fundamental rules in order for anything to happen and for it to start to fill up. The way Glinda works is that if there are multiples of something, not bound by any specific rule, there are an infinite number. So, out there is a universe, at least one, without a flaw or a flaw so small it never evolved. So it's empty.

Statistically, empty universes are uncommon, because there are a nearly infinite number of ways for a universe to be full but only one way to be completely empty. So, chosen at random, a universe is nearly infinitely many times more likely to have stuff than to have nothing. Which is good, because it's not a place I want to visit. In fact, fuck that place. Moving on.

## 3. Superstring Universes

If you take that same frazzled, overworked electron, and zoom in on it over and over and over again, you see that it's really made up of a bunch of strings, vibrating. These are called superstrings. The strings are too small to really be made out of anything. Which sounds like a cop out but it's true. They only have a single dimension, so, in all honesty, they are closer to ideas than things. And each one vibrates at a different frequency to make up all the different particles. So, even if you account for the quantized vibration rates, there are an infinite number of them with an infinite number of frequencies, making up a near infinite combination of worlds.

Most of these would make no sense to us at all. Like a universe with sentient colors, which I would call "Reading Rainbowland" If I could survive there for a picosecond. I could not.

## 4. Metaverses

If we accept that superstrings are real, even though they only have one dimension and are basically just an idea, we have to accept that, for the purposes of discussion, Metaverses exist. A Metaverse is a reality that is derived through fictional attribution, which means it's just made up.

This sounds absurd and non scientific, but imagine I'm telling a story about a slutty bear. In that story the bear is telling a story about a slutty girl who breaks into houses, eats porridge, and sleeps in beds. At some point, the girl tells a story about a slutty rabbit who races a slutty turtle. I don't know why they're all slutty, except maybe to say I might be a bit horny. At any rate, the Bear, the girl, the tortoise and the rabbit can't hang out and do stuff.

They are in different metaverses. Which sounds obvious, except these metaverses actually can influence each other, in some odd and recursive ways. This forces us to reconsider what real is, which isn't helping me get laid or put this cute halter type shirt on. So...

## 5. Paraverses

We can move things through time and space. In reality, they are similar things, dimensions just rotated. Pushing at an angle off of the time dimension can move you to a different timeline. But, for us, the other dimensions don't work that way. I can't push at an angle off of the width dimension to get to an alternate SPACE. But those spaces are there. They are called Paraverses and there are potentially an infinite number of them. There is even one where every word starts with the letter "P" because why the fuck not.

The far away ones have very different rules of physics. The nearby ones may have subtle differences. Like maybe you're a different gender and your name ends with a "a" and not an "o".

"So, I'm a Glissa, kula?" Soco pulled on a pair of leather pants.

Blu translated, "That means woman, here." I feel like I picked that one up from context.

Vietta replied, "Yes, that's a fairly small change. Gender's not a big deal. You might want to ask yourself why the girl version of you looks so much like Cheater Theater over here." She pointed at me as I finished putting on this cute halter top.

I gasped at her. "Are you saying we all look alike?"

"Reel it in, Dr. King. You're telling me you haven't noticed it?"

I tipped my head, "Well, she's a very pretty girl."

Albio looked at Soco. "I mean, she's hot?" Soco shrugged and nodded.

"I feel like wanting to fuck your genderswapped self is very emotionally healthy." I pulled on a pair of low rise shorts that showed a bit of pubic hair at top. I was now ready for church.

Kush agreed, "I would cluff gurka me so maxi" That sentence swirled out, floating up to the outer atmosphere and then finally fell back to earth, killing someone.

Blu shook her head. "I was not a cute little boy."

I tweaked her boobs from behind like I was a little bra. "But now you have these, which I'll hold on to for a moment if it's all the same to you."

"I'm trying to feel it out and see if we can jump timelines from here. I don't feel that wall." Albio lifted his head up. I didn't feel it, either, but I wanted to figure out what this world was before we started mucking around.

Vietta looked at him and scowled. I folded my arms, making it look like Blu was talking. "Hey, Albio was the one who figured out how to intentionally travel without drugs and sex. He knows what he's doing."

He winked at me, "yeah, why did we give up the drugs and sex part?"

I grabbed him and fixed his shirt. "Fuck if I know."I looked over to see Los was wearing a skirt. Not a huge selection of clothes here. "Can you spin a bit?"

He nodded and spun around. Undeniably very pretty. I suddenly missed my Davi and Sean. If we survived this with all our limbs I made a mental note to visit those fuckers.

Vietta snapped her fingers at me. I made another mental note to remove them all with a pinking sheers at the earliest opportunity. "Hey, Cheat Meat. She's coming back."

Brunhilda, super witch wasn't wrong.

Soca opened the tent door, "Did you find dripplies that fit?"

Blu turned to us, "That means - oh never mind." She sighed. It looks like this dimension spoke Junklish, too. I filed that word away to use when it wouldn't offend anyone.

I moved over to her, "Yes, thanks for the... Dripplies. I think we're just passing through."

She stared at me and Soco. "You two look like you could be frilkos. It's mawowzie."

I gestured for Soco to come over. "Yes, totally mawowzie. Maxi." I put their hands together to shake. And it happened. Soco's eyes began to glow blue again, not as strongly. But it was evident.

And so did hers.

I turned to everyone else, "You guys think that's cool, too, right? Let me do it again."

Everyone but Vietta and Albio nodded. I looked around. Where was Albio?

He pulled open the tent door and peered in. "Hey, guys. I think I need you to see this."

I opened the tent door and stepped out. It was still dark, but there were fires scattered around the tent. Beyond that it was hard to see but there were spotlights moving back and forth, occasionally illuminating the trees and other objects. And when they converged for a minute, we could see something bigger beyond it. It was nearly impossible to gauge how tall it was. But it was made out of some kind of metal and looked exactly how it did in that hologram.

A giant fucking statue of DAISY.

***

I left Carlos to watch over Soco, his ladyself, and Kush. Technically, this was a subtractionist only conversation, and while Los was one of us, he was so specialized that he rarely dealt with human beings, only animals.

And that's how he liked it.

We huddled around the fire as I looked around at them. "This isn't just a different timeline, this is a whole different paraverse. So how is Daisy here?"

Albio was nearly whispering, "Do the ordinarily discrete subtractionist databases include ways to travel to different paraverses?"

Vietta responded, "Not as such."

Blu nodded, "But they do include a database of known Zenakins."

That was scary, "So she got her own Zenakin."

Albio closed his eyes. I could tell he was following me. "If the zenakin are good guys, no one brought her here willfully." He looked scared.

Vietta offered, "What if she- it - lied to him/her. Them. The Zenakin."

Blu shook her head. "Based on my interactions, I don't see DAISY having the social acumen or the patience to lie."

"So what did she do to him?" I asked.

Albio pointed at the statue. "And that."

Again, I think he was thinking what I was thinking. Why the statue?

He continued, "A statue like that is pretty inefficient unless…"

Blu got it. "You're inspiring people with it."

He nodded, "People who worship power."

Vietta thought out loud, "ok, so maybe the Nasis with two 's'es back there are hers- being 'inspired'"

I leaned in, "right, but why START your own hate group, when it's more efficient to co-opt one?"

"So, it may be a different group here." Albio finished.

"Or we could be totally off base." Vietta picked up a rock and threw it. I understood her frustration. I still considered throwing the rock back at her head.

Los stepped past her. "It's almost time."

I looked around. Time for what?

Apparently, Soca had explained to everyone that the Chidis attack every morning at sun up here. Soco was no help as he and Kush didn't recognize that word. I had more questions than that. Like why were we being attacked at what looked like a game preserve? Who attacks in the morning? And how long had DAISY been here that she had time to build a big giant ass statue?

Suddenly, I heard movement in the forest around the tented areas. Soca pulled her people together and we all stood together near the opening.

Vietta stared forward and intoned, "They're here."

I rolled my eyes. "I'm so glad you're here and not rooting out missing children with the local constabulary like the other psychics."

"Eat me, Cheatapus."

"That's not a thing." It wasn't a thing.

But this was.

About two hundred people came running out of the forest. They were covered in dirt and mud and, as they got closer, I could see that they had shaved their teeth into points. For future reference, the people shaving their teeth into jagged little knife-like points are rarely the good guys.

As they started to swarm, Soco stepped up to knock them down while Albio, Blu, Vietta, and I started sending them elsewhere.

I looked over at Blu. They were very fast. "Where are you sending them?"

She shrugged. "I chose a place about 3 kilometers that way." She pointed.

Vietta spoke up, "They can probably do less damage if they're all scattered."

Albio nodded. I began to send them in all different directions. Soca's group had waded in to fight, but was mostly watching, overwhelmed by what was happening.

"Are you gabowing them?" she asked, her hand on my shoulder.

Blu yelled out. "Tell her we're not killing them."

I shook my head at Soca. Her people dove in, knocking the occasional one down while we played garbage men. Soca shouted out things to her men, about 40 or so people in mismatched outfits, uniforms and torn up rags. I realized that she had given us the best clothes she had. Blu exchanged a few words with her and then made her way to me.

Los moved over to the other side. He had been protecting Kush, who really didn't belong here. I put my arm around him.

Blu pointed toward the direction the Chidis had come from. "Soca says she wants us all to advance. This is the first time we have enough advantage to take the fight to them."

I nodded, "To DAISY." I waved to Soca to take the lead.

There were close to 50 of us, staying close, knocking out or disappearing the occasional chidi or small group we found on the way. They seemed animalistic, primitive. Apparently, in this dimension, Chidis were sort of primitivists, people adhering to some idea of what an alpha apex predator might be. They worshipped strength, which explained the massive statue. I shivered when I considered what DAISY might have had to do to get their allegiance. No doubt she killed quite a few of them.

Chidis made up most of this planet now, and the resistance was small. So far, we hadn't lost any. And I wanted to keep it that way. We tried to provide as much cover as possible. The statue seemed to get larger and more imposing as we got closer. At one point it threatened to blot out the sun behind it.

The tree cover thinned and we walked into an open field. A number of the errant chidis were standing in the field. They began to run toward us once they saw us. I disappeared a few at a distance as I felt the ground shake. Suddenly an area that looked to be about the size of a soccer pitch started to rise up from the ground. The chidis on top fell, with a few slipping into the sinkhole under it. They fell into the earth and disappeared.

The shape was a building, long and wide, only 20 or so meters tall, lights erupting all around us. For a moment, I was blinded until, reopening my eyes, I saw the half naked primitives pouring out the front. The building looked massive but simple.

Efficient.

A door opened in front, irising from the bottom, and a familiar shape stepped out in silhouette. I turned to Vietta next to me. "Look, it's little DAISY."

"Still ugly, " she shot back, noting the metallic reddish costume and sharply pointed ears over the rounded, elongated head.

She started walking forward and I noticed her gait. It was jerky, uneven. I realized I had never seen the DAISY avatar try to walk. Blu called out, "I need you to shut all this down. I cancelled the vacation project."

In a sensible multiverse, that would have been it. Daisy kept moving forward. "I hope you don't mind, Miss Aafjes, but I had already tabled that initiative."

Remembering last time, I put my hand out to the rest. Only subtractionists should talk to DAISY, I thought. "We want to shut down all the efficiency initiatives. Ok? Can we just do that?"

I looked around. I was being the reasonable one now. Who'd have thought that?

She paused for a minute and stopped walking. Then I heard a whirring sound and she continued. "I feel like all of us have sunk a great deal of effort into this, so if it's all the same to you, we'd like to continue."

One of the Chidis began running toward us. DAISY lifted her hand and exposed a dagger. A second later, the dagger appeared in his head. He kept running for a second or two on momentum, and then fell to the ground.

She looked at the body. "I didn't authorize that." Her head snapped up and she took in the group of us, subtractionists, Zenakins, and Resistance. For a moment, it looked like she was going to lift her hand again. Soca raised her gun and shot her in the head, sending part of her helmet flying.

DAISY looked at us. "I brought you to the failed timeline as a kindness so that I can eliminate it all at once, when I'm finished. Please have the courtesy and patience to stay where you are put."

She lifted the helmet to reveal a head. It was a suit. It was clear that the suit was talking. Because under it was a burned desiccated body, eyes blank and lifeless.

It was Soco.

I heard explosions as I turned around and then blackness.

## 11. Problematic Romances

I woke up surprised in Albio's lap. Apparently being right in front meant I would wake up later. The surprised part was why I was waking up at all. That little boobytrap was her chance to kill us all.

And she didn't take it.

Why not? Vietta smacked me on the head. She was apparently thinking the same thing. "Ok, she'll kill her own people but not us?"

Albio massaged my head. I preferred his way of getting my attention. "It's too much hassle to kill us? Or is there a kind of programmatic mandate against it?"

Blu wandered over. "I like that last idea. If it's true, it gives us an actual fighting chance."

Vietta sat down. "But, at the end, she can still eliminate the timeline we're in?"

Albio nodded. "That's kind of a loophole, maybe? So, the exploding mines just sent us back here, to start."

It had occurred to me that there might be another reason. "She's dressed like her weird ass approximation of a rat, right? What if she thinks she's one of us"

Blu looked inspired, "Right. That's useful."

I caught Los out of the corner of my eye, talking with Soco and Kush.

"Have any of you guys talked to him?"

"I was about to talk to him." Albio kept rubbing. And that's why I love him. "I mean, you guys saw what I saw, right?"

Vietta took a deep breath. "She's using a zenakin to travel, like we are. Except she's REALLY using him. His body."

Blue nodded, "And burning him out."

Albio leaned down and kissed me on the forehead. "C'mon. K. You and me."

He pulled me up and we walked over to Soco, pulling him aside. Albio patted him on the back. "Are you ok, man?"

He looked up. "Just kippie." I assumed that either meant he was all right or that he was a giant fish. I took a whiff and decided it was the former.

Albio let out a big breath. "You saw that, right?"

"So, that was a kiriglo axmo of me?

Those were some ugly words, I thought. "Yeah, she must have gotten another version of you from a different timeline and plugged him in. I mean you in."

"How did she find me... I mean him?"

This was the elephant in the room. "That's why I wanted to talk to you. I think we led her to you. There are 17 other Zenakins on your earth. I actually can do the math on that one. There is a 5.88% chance it was random." I tried to catch his eye. "It's my fault."

He hugged me and lifted me up. "No."

And then he kissed me for about a minute. Which was a far better response than the one I thought I'd get. I kissed him back and thought for a bit. Grabbing both the guys' hands, I returned to the group.

"I say we spend the night and help Soca fight them off again in the morning before we try to slide timelines. It's sort of the least we can do for her."

Vietta agreed. "We don't need to confront captain quickbooks again."

"Agreed," shot back Blu.

Albio thought for a second and commented, "And she's speaking in the plurality of royalty now."

I considered that, "Do you think she's in contact with her other selves?"

I looked over at Vietta and she laughed. "I would. Why the hell not?"

We helped Soca's team clean up and do some chores. She was glad to have our help, especially since she anticipated a bigger attack than usual in the morning. I looked around at her bedraggled group and felt her sense of hopelessness. She was trying, despite the impossibility of it all. She was one of those leaders that did the dishes with everyone else after dinner, so I joined her. With me drying, it went lightning fast.

Kush took Albio and Vietta off to a tent to film some stuff for her channel as the rest of us hung out around the fire, watching the sun start to slowly go down. Of all of us, she was the only one who'd managed to hold on to her phone as we slid here. Soco tried dancing with his other self around the fire but the blue light kept returning every time they touched. I realized that this would be a major impediment to this idea of fucking your gender swapped self.

I imagined starting a star crossed romance with someone who, every time you tried to make out with them, lit up like a sparkler and sucked you into a whirlpool portal to another world. This was something couples therapy couldn't really fix.

I grabbed Soco and danced close with him for a little bit. He had every right to be pissed at me for putting him and every other version of him in danger. But he wasn't. He just wanted to save his world. And he was grateful to have that chance. When the sun went down you could see every star. I noticed that they were mostly where they belonged for this time. This timeline - and this paraverse - wasn't so far away that the astronomical configuration was substantially different.

The area around the fire began to thin out as I dragged Soco back to the tent we were assigned. Vietta, Albio, and Kush were asleep naked on a mattress with him in the center. Vietta was holding him, her face in his neck, while Kush was inverted, her pussy in his face, and her hands holding on to his cock. It looked like they had all fallen asleep in the middle of sex. I thought about how to place the blanket and decided that Kush would have to be totally covered. It looked messy but warm. Goodnight, greenie. I hope you're a strong breather.

I reached over to her phone, propped up on a trunk and turned it off. Laying it flat, I pulled Soco over to another mattress. I slid my shorts off and laid down next to him, talking. We lay on our back, me with one leg over his and the over off the mattress as he fingered me and told me all about himself. We joked about the kinds of superheroes we'd want to be and what we would do to fix our ridiculous timelines.

He moved his fingers in me as I turned my head to look right at him. I felt myself wet around his hand as he ran his thumb over my clit, massaging it softly. He was on his left side now, rubbing me and fingering me with his right hand while I spread my legs as wide as they could go. I thought about myself as an electrical socket, open and available, while the wires of his fingers plugged into me, creating a connection.

My head leaned as right as it could, putting my eyes only inches away from his. He dug his fingers in even deeper, creating a rhythm that seemed to sync with my heartbeat. I arched my back and moaned, reaching my tongue out to lick his pretty lips while he talked. I pressed my left hand on my belly, right below my belly button, to feel the machine-like movement of his fingers. I pushed down, closing my eyes. I felt the muscles in my ass tighten as a light spray poured out of me. I breathed out and came.

I took a beat after cumming for the first time as I told him the one word from his timeline that I had actually developed a fondness for. Out of all the other semantic abortions, this one I loved. And I wanted to bring back with me when we got home.

He slid his fingers deeper in me and kept massaging until finally climbing on top of me.

And I called him "Nexty."

Neighbor.

***

I grabbed Albio in the morning to help me make breakfast. He and I had cooked together a lot and we kind of had a shorthand that couldn't be replaced. He had spent the morning placing weapons all over and wanted to tell me where they all were. I had to admit that Albio was a good past self. I looked over at him in his "kiss the "grielko" apron, looking absurd.

"Looking good, Alan."

He laughed. "Uh oh."

"What?"

"You call me Alan like twice a year when you're feeling weepy."

"I am not feeling weepy."

"I'm sure you aren't."

"If anything, YOU'RE feeling weepy, Alan Biolensky."

"I am?"

"I had to suffocate the green girl last night. Almost killed her with a blanket. I know you're upset."

"I am traumatized, you blanket wielding maniac."

"I just wanted to say something serious for a second."

He looked at me. "That's fair. The last one was me. So, go for it." He crossed his arms and leaned against the makeshift grill. I had just a second before the bacon burned.

"I just wanted to say…" For a second, I had the instinct to make a joke out of it. I squashed that instinct like an overstuffed ant after an unprotected jelly candy picnic.

"I just wanted to say that loving you makes it easy for me to love everything else and thank you…for that."

He smiled at me and wiped his hands. "Can I tell you a story?"

I nodded.

"On my first solo mission, I was bringing a cancer cure back to an earlier timeline."

For reference, this is everyone's first solo mission. So I was not looking surprised yet. I gave him a "go on" look. Bacon was cooking.

"Like everyone does. And at the research center, I met a kid, on the way out. A girl. She was drawing a picture for her mom. In it was the little girl but her mom was huge, like a big round planet. Her mom asked her to explain the picture."

I put my hands around him. "Ok, we're getting somewhere I know it."

He continued, "And she said. - I love you, but the 'you'- the mom, in the picture - was everything. She was her day and night and her protector and her best friend. Her mom was everything. So, when she said 'I love you…'"

I kissed his neck. "I get it. You think I've gained a little weight."

"She was saying, 'I love everything.' And that's how her mom gave the world to her. And let her love the world. It's how YOU give me the world."

"Uggh, this romance thing is hard," I whined.

He fixed my hair around my face a little and whispered. "It's so hard."

He kissed me. He smelled like bacon, which was a kind of win, too.

The camp alarm went off not long after.

This gave us 20 minutes to get ready for this attack. An attack at the same time every day was efficient, but it wasn't very logical. Why do this? DAISY didn't care about the people she lost. Maybe this was about locking the remaining people into HER schedule. So they knew it would happen every day. And had to be ready.

Every day.

I think I was starting to figure out how DAISY thought- how she worked. For the record, that's always the point where shit gets scary. I tried not to get over confident.

We moved outside to the edge of the camp. I grabbed Vietta and Blu. "Can you guys feel a path to a different timeline here in this paraverse?

Vietta nodded, "I think so. And I think I know which one. Our best bet is to go back to a timeline before the birth of English. Then we follow forward to Blu's timeline."

"Where everyone speaks Dutch." She interjected.

"And," Vietta continued, "we get back to Soco's lifetime and cross over to another paraverse from there."

I got it, "Because there will be another Soco. Got it." We needed a time when he was alive. A Zenakin can't go to a paraverse where a version of him/her doesn't exist.

"Ok, I like it." Then, after we aren't boxed in, we can go to headquarters, make a complaint and get DAISY wiped.

"Which they should be able to do if they go back early enough." Blu finished.

It seemed like everyone was on the same page. Now we just had to vanish a few Chidis, Clean up after breakfast and scoot. I was almost back to feeling like I had a handle on all this.

Almost.

So we waited. And then we waited a little bit longer.

Soca began to look alarmed. For over a year, there had been an attack at the same time every day. It had whittled her people down, forced them into this bizarre 24 hour planning cycle.

And now, the day after we brought the fight directly to DAISY, no attack.

Blu looked all around. "Does anyone else think this is actually worse?"

She wasn't wrong. It was so much worse.

I moved around the perimeter. Was there a chance they would come from a different direction today? All of it seemed to stupid. During the American Revolution, British soldiers fought the war in the traditional way that warfare had been waged up until then. They stood at attention, lined up and shot, then reloaded as the other side had their chance to shoot. It was remarkably stupid and it encouraged the American colonists to "cheat" by learning from the indigenous people how they fought.

I'll give you a guess, but it wasn't walking in from the front in a straight line and waiting for their asses to get shot.

I started to feel like that's what we were doing. We were just sitting there, with the entire rest of the world knowing where we were and DAISY plotting over all of it.

After another half hour, Soca and the rest of us got together and tried to figure it out, with the rest of the group playing lookout.

Vietta started, "ok, DAISY doesn't care anymore since it knows we haven't left, thinks we can't leave and being trapped in this failed timeline in this paraverse is no different than being trapped in that one." She pointed. I tried to imagine where she thought she was pointing.

Blu nodded, "Yeah, that's where I'm at."

Soca looked around at us, "Failed…"

I tried to explain that DAISY considered all of this to be sort of collateral in its war to make things more efficient.

Albio started, "We still think all the versions of it are connected, right?"

"I think so." Honestly, I don't see why not. It sounded like it. And its use of "We" kept coming back to me. For our part, we kept alternating between calling it a her hand her an it.

He continued, "So, it doesn't matter where we are. As long as we don't get back to the main timelines, we don't matter."

That definitely rubbed at me the wrong way. I got dressed for this. To be told I don't matter sucked.

I heard a noise in the distance. It sounded like it might have been a tiny aircraft taking off. Something supersonic. I turned toward Soca and the sound increased in volume, ramping up incredibly quickly.

It was a scream.

Her lieutenant was standing right next to her. I tried to remember his name as he exploded violently, sending blood and entrails all over the ground, splattering Soca and those of us nearest.

He had been hit by something falling from the sky.

I moved closer. There were two skulls in the mess on the ground, surrounded by shattered bones and gunk.

A falling chidi.

I looked up into the sundrenched sky. We could hear that sound all around us. They were falling all around us, raining down.

While we stood there, trying to figure out which direction they would come from, DAISY was dropping her followers on us like hailstones, smashing into tents, into people, destroying the few structures around us that Soca's group had managed to build.

We scattered. The screams became louder and thicker, as falling Chidis filled the air above us. Blu, Vietta, Albio and I started vanishing them as fast as we could, but they were impossibly numerous. The sun was blotted out by them as, one by one, the people around us were smashed to the ground. The air was brown with blood and body parts, filtering into the space around us. Los worked hard to protect Soco and Kush, pulling them under him as he waved to the sky, trying to catch them all and send them away.

They would retain their velocity, no matter what we did. Sending them anywhere was as much of a death sentence as letting them fall here. Their screams were horrific and the sounds of impact were even worse. For a second, I lost track of our group and couldn't see Albio or Blu anywhere. I lifted my hands and tried to focus on moving them all away as one big group.

Then, as suddenly as it started, it was over. The air was deadly quiet. Soca had lost over half her people. Los stepped over with Kush and Soco. I looked to my left and could see Soca, and the rest of our team. We were covered in blood and parts, slipping on the ground that was blood-muddy and thick with bones and pieces of skin and clothing.

There were tears in Soca's eyes. I stepped toward her and she shook her head. She was staring over my shoulder.

I turned around to see DAISY walking, in that jerky and near-mechanical stride, into the clearing. The whirring and clanking from its awkward suit was the only sound left in that opening. I turned toward the thing as it spoke.

"Pardon the mess. There is a lesson here. I learned, over years, to listen to my programming and to, essentially, follow orders. This is what made me good at what I did. You…" It waved. "All of you have not yet learned how to follow orders. And this poor woman here…" He pointed at Soca. "It's her people that paid for that. I mean, I think that is worth an apology."

I was breathing hard. I thought about calling out, asking this thing to stop.

At that moment, there was nothing I could say that wouldn't make it worse. Nothing that would make it stop.

Soco moved over toward me. DAISY's eyes followed him. "You." DAISY shook its head. "Excuse me for a moment." The suit opened and the dried up, dead version of Soco dropped to the ground. Just as quickly, it sealed back up again. DAISY stepped toward us, leaving the body behind to rot on the ground.

It was walking perfectly now.

"I think we can say that this is done now." Daisy began to raise its hand. Soca leaped in front of Soco, pushing him back, and the jagged edge of a knife appeared, sticking out of her throat. Her blood spurted straight ahead out as her eyes widened.

I heard DAISY call out "oh, people, that was uncalled - " as Soca lifted her hand and the blue light surrounded us. The red mud below us shifted and swirled, faster than I could hold on, pulling us down, away. I slid below the mud.

 I never heard the next word.

## 12. Potential Superheroes

I hit the ground hard on my back, knocking the wind out of me for a second. I pulled myself up, grabbing Soco's hand. "Try again. Now, back."

He closed his eyes and I could see his forehead furrow as he made the effort.

Nothing.

He tried again. Harder,.

I stood up and kicked at the dirt under us. We were scattered across an open clearing. He was trying as hard as he could. And it wasn't working. "Try again."

Vietta came up behind me and grabbed my arm. "Stop."

I pushed her away and leaned into Soco, "Again…"

He shook his head. "It's not working…"

Vietta put her arms around me. She was covered in blood and gunk, just like I was. I remembered what a joke it was the last time we were like this. The last time we were covered in a mess like this. My knees hit the ground.

I heard Kush ask, "why…?"

Blu's voice answered, "A Zenakin can only travel to their own home, or a paraverse with a… living version of them."

I pulled Soco over to me and hugged him.

We cried on the dirt and grass covered in the blood of little monsters from a world we could never go back to.

Los was only inches away from him and Kush, as he had been since this whole thing started. I got up and pulled him aside.

"Carlos. Your first instinct has been to protect Kush and Soco and I get that. Please don't think I'm shutting you out. I'm relying on you to keep doing that. I trust your instincts to protect more than anything. You know that, right?"

He leaned in and touched his forehead to mine, whispering, "I get it. I got this."

If he weren't completely covered in gook, I would have kissed him. Los was a protector. This is what he did. I saw that now. He did it so that I didn't have to think about what bullshit I dragged these people into.

I heard a woman's voice from behind me. I turned to see a pretty blonde woman addressing Soco. "What's going on? What's that Fleckum?"

He looked at me and then at her. "I'm not who you think I am."

She shook her head. Well, whoever you are, do you all want to come get rorokeled?"

***

20 minutes later we were hosing ourselves off in a fenced in yard behind a single family home that seemed to be very heavily fortified, or at least as highly secure as a home on this earth at this time could be. With this level of technology.

The fence itself was metal and thick wood and was probably 10 meters high. It wrapped all around us with a gate in front and one in back that seemed to lead off into a forest.

The skies were slightly reddish and I had no idea why.

The blonde woman, whose name was Klar, folded her arms and stared at us as she tried to get a grip on what we'd told her.

"Ok, gribble me if I've gotten this maxi kippie. You are my giffili's houfili, whose gadgeo is also Soco, and these are your Grilliwigs you've been boroking with until your van crashed into a kludgem in a nearby kurfuka?"

I looked over. "Mawowzie." This is a word I had in my back pocket. I'm pretty sure it meant "Amazing." As for the rest, I was hoping there was a pig farm somewhere around here that explained this. We looked like animated bratz dolls used as strawberry jam spoons by toddlers. And Soco being his own cousin was not something I would have tried. It felt dirty and inbred.

Soco stared as we all washed each other off. Klar's problem was she didn't know where her husband was. Given that DAISY seemed to be connected across the timelines and paraverses, I had a bad feeling about that.

A siren went off. Out of instinct I looked up and saw a series of planes overhead. Klar spat out. "Curfew. You have to bracko."

We heard noises from the front. Klar ducked into her house, leaving us to fend for ourselves. The noise was coming from the front fence. It sounded like banging at the fence, some kind of machinery slamming into it. The noise got louder and more rhythmic. It was definitely machinery. The side fences were shaking and buckling, too. I looked around the group and pointed to the back of the yard. We all moved backward, watching the fences shake. Suddenly a human sized hole appeared in the back of the house as some kind of explosion ripped open the third floor.

Vietta made it to the back fence first, kicking open the gate. The siren seemed louder once we were past the gate into the forest. I looked at Soco who motioned us to the left. We started running through the forest, still mostly covered in goo. There was a swoosh in the air above us, as though one of the planes had flown too low. We ducked and kept running.

There was a clearing ahead. We ran up to the clearing and then, looking up, carefully stepped into it. About 50 meters away was a wall, covered in decorations of some sort, colorful, like flags. As we got closer, we could see that they weren't flags.

Hanging from the walls were hundreds of people. Hundreds of dead bodies. Each one had drawn that symbol on their shirts or chests, in blood, paint, whatever was available, apparently

DAISY'S symbol. The twisted rat face.

Kush started crying as Blu looked at their faces. Blu's voice cracked. "There. That's Ebony Contrales. That's Even Range. These are subtractionists." She looked back at me. "Some of these are my friends."

Vietta mouthed, "Fuck." I kept my face down. I didn't need to see who I knew was up there.

I whispered loudly. "Back to the tree line." and we all started to run. The trees got closer as I heard a sound, again, like a jet plane. I didn't have time to look up as the sound stopped, leaving a man standing right in front of us. He was a dark skinned black man in a blue suit with the letters "PG" on front in a stylized yellow emblem, a yellow cape, and something over one eye. We stopped as he moved forward, slowly, casually.

It was Soco.

As he approached, he was talking. We could hear it all around us. It was reverberating from the trees. It was in our heads. It was his lips moving but it was DAISY'S mechanized voice.

"Blu Aafjes, honestly, I had thought you and your friends could wait this out in your nice hottub until I needed you. We're getting some excellent work done. Really fine stuff."

The device attached to his face looked like a piece of some futuristic radio with tendrils that reached into his eye socket and stabbed into his brain. He kept advancing.

"I need you to say your respects to your friends and then skee-daddle, if you can. We have a lot to do." He scanned us and seemed to focus on Soco and Kush.

"Don't need you." Almost too fast to see, he flew toward them and disappeared.

Vietta looked at me. "Where?"

I started moving toward the tree line again, with everyone behind me. "Exact opposite side of the planet."

We ran into the forest until we couldn't see the wall anymore and stopped.

I turned to everyone. "Ok, what did we just learn?"

Albio shot out. "DAISY has its own superhero."

Vietta continued. "Her. I know we go back and forth, but the voice is female. The shape of the armor last time, the statue, even the drawing. Feels female. We have to think of her the way she thinks of herself to understand her."

I nodded, "Agreed."

Blu added, "I think Soca tried to send us to the place with the strongest version of her."

Albio looked sad, "She died thinking she wasn't strong enough to help us."

Soco was still scanning the skies. "That's me, kula."

It was. "Yep. A superhero."

Suddenly we heard a voice. I looked over to see Klar huddled behind a tree. She looked hurt. Los ran over and kneeled down.

She continued sadly, "That's PaxiGurka." The greatest hero ever. My giffili"

Los looked at me and shook his head. I knelt down next to him.

All of her ribs were broken and she was bleeding inside everywhere. It was a miracle she'd gotten this far into the forest.

She looked up. "I used to currrihuri that sound. Wooosh." She closed her eyes.

"I tried to feel my way inside her, like I did for Los. There was nowhere to start. She was already dead, she just didn't know it. Her body didn't realize it yet.

Soco stepped over and held her hand, kissing it as she stopped breathing. He never met her but this was a person who loved a version of him, right up until the end.

I stood up and moved toward the largest tree. Albio and Vietta followed. "Now when we get that fucking thing off of the other Soco, we have to tell him he killed his wife."

Albio leaned in. "I tried to send the device somewhere. It wouldn't go. Did you guys feel that?"

Vietta nodded, "Me, too. While he was yapping." She made a yapping motion with her hand.

Blu walked over. "PaxiGurka. PowerMan. He's strong. He can fly, obviously."

I put my hand into Blu's and closed my eyes. "Did you see Davi up there? I didn't look, I can't…"

Blu grabbed my face, "No, Kerys, she's not. She's not up there. No versions of her. I promise."

I leaned into her. I felt like there was a big pit ready to open up in front of me. It would feel so good to just fall into it.

Vietta took a breath, "Why AREN'T we back in a hot tub right now? No, hear me out. She's been trying to keep us away from something she's doing. Why us? Why not just kill us? She's trying to create efficiency. All I've seen her do is kill people so far."

Vietta knew i needed this, I think,

I started, "ok, on a certain level, maximum efficiency could be attained if everyone were dead."

Albio offered up, "Like an empty universe?"

I continued, "It depends on what you think of as efficiency. But that is an example of a very efficient universe." I thought for a second. But was it really? I started thinking about the definition of efficiency.

Blu thought for a second, "In that body, it looks like he can kill subtractionists. And he wanted to kill these two, who aren't." She pointed to Kush and Soco.

Vietta finished, "But she as much as said directly she'll be needing us."

I tried to work it out. It didn't really make any sense. "What does she need US for? Why US and not them?"

Blu stared back toward the wall. "Or them."

\*\*\*

We knew PaxiGurka was going to find us eventually anyway but there was no reason we had to make it easy for him. Kush mentioned that, in her paraverse, there was a hotel two states over where she used to shoot content at that was undergoing renovation. There wouldn't be any customers and, on the weekend, like today, there might not be much construction. So we shuttled ourselves there.

This might give us an hour or two to get cleaned up and relax before PaxiGurka realized he could zone in on Soco as a Zenakin. But it worked two ways. Soco could tell where the superhero was, too.

If he was awake. And alive.

We grabbed a couple of large connecting rooms on the 30th floor so we could stay close, and washed ourselves off, washing clothing in the sinks. Only one of the connecting rooms had power, which was odd, but the television worked.

I sat naked on the couch with Soco, cleaning my boots while our clothes soaked. Blu, Albio, and Kush were doing a circuit through the building to see if they could find any food. Soco sat in a hotel robe thumbing through channels.

We learned a bit.

DAISY seemed to have been here on this planet for a while. My guess was that she had gone back and been here for at least a year. During that time she had wiped out most of the planetary leaders, installing the one or two superheroes that she could find on the planet as their replacements. It looked like there were three major ones, each with a device on their heads, like PaxiGurka.

Martial Law had been declared across the major countries, all of whom seemed to be in a holding pattern, waiting for war or for Insurrection, or something. No one seemed to know what they were waiting for.

Los and Vietta came in from the shower with towels on. He sat on the floor between my legs. While she slid onto the wide white couch next to Soco. I felt bad that Soco would have to stay awake and feel for the other version of himself while we took turns sleeping.

I looked down and thought that it might be a good time to actually shave. The thick bush I had grown at the beginning of time was even slightly thicker, giving Carlos' face a comical bearded appearance as I pulled his face in to lick me. Vietta climbed on top of Soco's lap, facing him, and called out "oh, DJ Chris," theatrically. We all laughed gratefully as the news went on in a surreal display of pretend normalcy. Reading between the lines it was clear the entire world had been taken over by this artificially polite mad entity but no one seemed much to care. And I struggled to see how any of it was more efficient.

The stories were small, banal, average. The pundits waved their arms around talking about nothing while global events squeaked by. Inefficiently.

We had closed the blinds in the hotel suite but we could still tell it was getting dark. I tried to relax but the sound of that "woosh" kept clawing through my head. Los' tongue on me helped, for sure, but a part of my brain still tried to figure it out. The idea of efficiency was not complex. It describes how well a system turns input energy into output labor or energy without waste. Waste could be heat or energy loss to friction or anything.

I thought about Carlos working between my legs, his energy, nearly all of it, converted to my pleasure. I put my hand on his head and pressed myself harder into his face. He knew me well enough that there was little wasted energy. I could feel how badly he loved this, how much he wanted it. His passion for tasting me, for wanting his face in me, it added energy to the system.

It added everything.

I started breathing a little harder. This is right when he would become an animal. This is where his brain shut off and he would just eat at me, dig into me with his mouth, because he couldn't stop. This is when the energy of his labor became negligible. He couldn't tell because sucking me, running his tongue across my clit as he drank me, there was no effort needed for him. He was tapping into something else.

Vietta grabbed my tits and held on while Soco came inside her. She moaned lazily and squeezed me hard. I grabbed her hair and kissed her, feeling the sweat on her neck while I licked at it. I bit her neck hard, like I used to in school, and heard the wet smacks of her cumming on his dick.

That may have pushed me over the edge. It added energy to my own act. Suddenly, I felt myself cumming in Los' face. He stopped for a moment and breathed. I grabbed his hair and dragged him between Soco's legs. He started cleaning up Soco's cock with his mouth as I pulled Vietta over onto my lap and kissed her.

I pushed her head between my legs and placed her knees on opposite sides of my neck, one on each shoulder. Dipping my face into her cunt in front of me I could lick the warm cum from it while she slithered down my belly, sucking my wet pussy. I slid down on the couch a little and found the perfect spot where I didn't have to move my head at all in order to feel her dripping into my mouth.

Was any of this efficient? The output was significant. The energy that came from it was intoxicating. It was powerful. And the input was seemingly negligible. I barely had to move my neck to reach all of Vietta's parts, scooping out the warmth of Soco's orgasm and devouring her. Carlos lazily brought Soco's cock back to life, giving it a new power, a new authority, as he slowly fucked his mouth.

Nothing made sense. Were humans inefficient or were we hyper efficient? The work it took Vietta to suck on my clit, to bite my lips in just the right way, to lose herself in my cunt, it was nothing to her. What was energy that we HAD to give off. It was heat.

It was waste.

This was how the heat waste of living was expended. And turned into life. I hear Albio, Blu, and Kush walk in, putting down their finds on the counter as they made their way over the couch to join us. I heard Kush giggle as she watched the system, the rule, of humanity.

This was human efficiency. Nothing DAISY was doing was really efficient. Because none of it was permanent. And, at the end, I suspected none of it would matter.

It would disappear. It was a means to an end.

I squeezed my legs and finished again on Vietta's face. I hugged her tightly and rested my face on her cunt. She still tasted like a bad person, but Soco's cum made it better. Besides, even bad people can taste good sometimes. I considered that as an ad campaign. I filed it away for copyright purposes.

The TV was off when we came up for air.

Albio handed me a bag of Velkru flavored cookies, on which I took a chance.

It was cinnamon.

I pulled my knees up. I looked up at Albio and Blu. "None of this is her plan. And she doesn't want an empty universe. And an empty universe really isn't efficient, either."

Blue popped a chip in her mouth. "What does she want?"

"She wants to change the rules. For everything."

I wondered for a second if I was tired.

"I think."

# 13. Powerman and the Legion of Blah Blah Blah

**Subtractionist First Level Written Test**

**Section 1. Psychological and general aptitude.**

*Answer the following questions as honestly as you can. Please make an effort not to spend too much time thinking about each one. It is more helpful to us to have your immediate responses, authentic and natural. The questions are phrased in a conversational way to encourage a conversational response. Moving along.*

**Question 1:**

Hey. Let's say, for argument's sake, you have friends. Would these friends say that you are the kind of person who is capable of having fun no matter where you are, no matter the situation?

**Question 2:**

Quickly, name 7 or more of these friends who are not imaginary who would say this about you. Faster.

**Question 3:**

In one paragraph or less, describe your general methodology for talking to people who don't speak your language or think you are just a huge fucking idiot.

**Question 4:**

For each term, please describe your quick, immediate response to being called that term by a new friend you just met.

A: Butch

B: Wizard

C: Fuckcandy

D: Lil' Flower

E: Great God(dess) of the skies

F: Peachy

G: Mommy/Daddy

H: Demon God(dess)

**Question 5:**

Describe your favorite kind of day in one paragraph or less. Describe the people around you.

**Question 6:**

Describe, in one paragraph or less, what happens if you are having the kind of day outlined in question 5 and everything explodes. During the explosion, whom do you save first? Name Names.

**Question 7:**

Please provide the punchlines for these jokes:

A: Why did the pirate want to travel to Proxima Centauri?

B: Why did the Higgs Boson go to church?

C: Why is it hard to date a topological insulator?

D: What do you get when you cross a mountain climber with a mosquito?

E: What did Heisenberg say when the cop stopped him and told him how fast he was going?

F: What did the Lesbian Physicist do today?

G: What did the helium atom do when the bartender called him a noble gas?

**Question 8:**

Describe, in a paragraph or less, the way each of these items functions and how you might build or make it with limited materials:

A: A coherent Light Gun

B: A Mass Reactor Generator

C: A Large Scale Particle Replicator

D: A Terrestrial Radio

E: A Pair of glasses

F: A Diaper

G: Ravioli al uovo

H: a 21st century cell phone cloner

I: A cute club-ready halter top

J: A ceramic projectile weapon

K: a small yield alcubierre bubble space weaving bomb

L: Shoe polish

M: Gum

N: Pthallo Green Acrylic paint

O: A space-reaching satellite response system

P: A rope ladder

Q: A zine

R: Seitan

S: Brunch for 20 people

## Question 9:

Would you say you are comfortable with living under different customs and moral codes without being judgmental or a whiny little bitch? Would you like to get a drink later?

## Question 10:

Would you say that you are an honest person, but enjoy telling lies sometimes when it's necessary as long as no one gets hurt? When are we getting that drink?

**Question 11:**

Do you like to lead, but also to follow someone smart but sometimes be alone until you are around people and then you enjoy their company until they leave and then you maybe don't know when they're coming back but you're ok with it?

**Question 12:**

In one paragraph or less, who is your favorite character to play if you were in a play and why. Why is that character the hero? What kind of drink are we having? Does it matter? I'm okay if it's just a late dinner.

**Question 13:**

In one paragraph or less explain why your favorite time travel movie is completely reasonable and makes perfect sense from a hard physics perspective. Lie if you have to, but do it well. Do you want to watch it with me?

**Question 14:**

Do you have a preferred effective masturbation technique if you had to be alone for the rest of your life in a world devoid of electricity or facilitative sex devices? Explain in a paragraph or less. Do you think this test is hitting on you? If yes, please write in your full phone number.

**Question 15:**

What would you do, in a paragraph or less, if someone elected you president of earth as a joke, but you couldn't resign?

**Question 16:**

You are given a calf skin wallet as a welcome gift by a man in a strange tribe. You look at him and his face is vaguely cow-like. He asks you to put something in the wallet while he watches. In one paragraph or less, you respond...

**Question 17:**

For how long do you think you could successfully pretend to be a stupid person?

**Question 18:**

On a scale from 0 to 10, how fundamentally evil do you think human beings are at birth, with 0 being not evil at all and 10 being maximally evil.

**Question 19:**

Can you answer the same question for:

A: Bobcats

B: Ocelots

C: Camels

D: Sharks

E: Gum

**Question 20:**

If you were the last person alive, how long would you want to live? Explain.

If you read this far, you probably want to know my answers to Question 7. I carry them with me in my head and shall never forget. In order:

A: To spend some time at c

B: For mass

C: They're all surface

D: Nothing, you can't multiply a scalar and a vector

E: Fuck, now, I'm lost

F: Double Slit experiment

G: Nothing. He didn't react

These are the first 20 questions you get in written form, when you apply to be a subtractionist. This is to get past the first level. There are SO MANY more. I supply these to you for context. I think they might help explain to you what KIND of people we are. Eventually, you can recognize that kind of person. Can we generally have fun anywhere and at any time? Yes. Are we able to live in cultural gray zones? Also yes. Are we ok in groups and alone? Yes indeed. Are we easily offended? No. Are we usually the kinds of people who throw ourselves into the shit at all times.

Yes.

But I had passengers now. People who never took that test and had to explain in some twisted paragraph what they would do if they had to masturbate at the end of the world or some such shit.

Kush had seen nightmares in the last couple of days. And Soco had literally watched two versions of himself die and one taken over by some insane robot intelligence.

Albio and the others were hanging out, talking with and listening to Soco in the other room while I sat in the hotel bathtub with Kush, candles all over, brushing her shock of pale green hair and talking with her, through the incomprehensible words, to make sure she was ok. I didn't really need her to take a 20 question test to figure out what kind of person she was.

She liked her life. She liked her friends. She liked her freedom. I imagined her taking requests from men on the internet and feilding even the most ridiculous ones. She would smile and say, "Well, I'm not going to do that, but I'll do this, how's that?" and they would agree because she would be right. Her idea was more beautiful. It was more worth doing.

She was the girl who would do handstands in a skirt after school for the boys but walk away if they said something stupid. She'd pull her tits out for people driving by in a car but not if it was a married couple who might fight about it. The kind of girl who made friends easily and then forgave them until they figured out how to be better people. She didn't deserve to be watching dead people hanging on a wall or primitive warrior people dropped from out of the sky or any of this shit.

We laughed while we moisturized each other after stepping out of the bath. If you've ever had a moisturizing buddy you know it's so much better than doing it yourself. And we shaved each other. That was a long time coming. But we were fresh and hairless stepping out of the bathroom, just as horny porno jesus demanded.

I remembered reading a story when I was younger about why Batman had a robin. I mean, why would someone like Batman need a kid to tag along and help?

It was because Batman needed a reminder of why he did what he did. He needed this innocent kind kid, willing to fight, to show him that there were people worth fighting for. No matter how ugly things got, he just needed to turn to the left and see a good, kind person. Someone he could fight for.

Kush was just a good person. It would never cross her mind to be mean or cruel. And if she had appeared in a hot tub anywhere on my world, she would have gotten along just fine.

Not just because she was cute as fuck, but because it was obvious about her. My guess is that she would have giggled her way through the psych part of the subtractionist test and come out with high marks. That's why this was going to work.

Yes, I thought this timeline was absurd and semantically distressing. But everytime I heard DAISY call it a "failed timeline" I imagined Kush being phased out of existence and I wasn't about to let that happen. Certainly not by some poorly designed UX nightmare of a robot bookkeeping program who couldn't even half-ass plan a vacation. Even if it HAD learned how to time travel.

Except.

How did it?

I grabbed Kush and we stepped into the other room. It was bright, even though the shades were drawn. We'd been hanging out entirely by candle light.

Albio smiled, "whoa. No more bushes."

I curtseyed politely. Kush did a little spin and showed off her freshly shaved self. This was fun but not the point.

I started, "Hey, guys, let me ask you a question." I slid into a bar seat around the counter, still butt ass naked as god and the millions of viewers of Cluff Waterbubblecup intended.

Vietta passed me a drink and cocked her head. "You had to shave to ask a question? Kind of extra, I think."

"Yes I did. VIETTA. I really did." I countered. "Answer me this. We learned how to time travel by recognising the beauty of the universe and that it had a kind of will and wanted to have that beauty recognized and seen."

Albio nodded. "Exactly."

Blu agreed, "Yes, that's it."

I continued, "Does DAISY seem like a beauty recognizing sort of gal?"

Vietta took a breath. "Ok, no. But she's using Zenakins to travel laterally, through the paraverses. What if she's using subtractionist brains or something to travel in time?"

"We would see that, right? The one she was using?" I asked.

Blu looked around the counter at us. "I think so."

Vietta took a big chug of orange juice they had found in a fridge downstairs. "The test."

Albio had taken the test most recently. He'd only been a subtractionist for about two years, his personal time. "The test selects for a certain kind of person."

I looked over at Soco and Kush. "We take an initial test to become one of these rat things. The psychological part is woven into all of it. They want to make sure that we are people who know how to have fun, no matter where we are, in case we end up lost in some random timeline and have to blow up a three legged cow for entertainment."

Vietta raised her glass. "To T-bone. You was a good aminal." There may have been some vodka in that orange juice.

I poured one out for T-bone and went on. "The psych part of the test also pretty much ensures that you see the universe as a good place. That you like people and don't really want to hurt them. And besides this one here, I DON'T want to hurt anyone. And I don't think someone who passed that test could drop living human beings on people."

Blu continued, "You're right. And I don't think anyone who learned how to travel like we did would have failed that test."

Albio nodded, "So, she is using old technology to travel, or..."

Los had been trying to get a kernel of popcorn into his mouth from a height. He was always so quiet, you could forget he was there. "She split her brain."

Albio shook his head confused.

Blu looked excited. "Discrete. It's in her name. She wanted to be able to do terrible things. For efficiency. But she needed to learn how to travel. So she split up her brain. Part of it loves this universe, loves the world. Thinks that people are good."

"And part of it is an evil goosestepping piece of hot slimy mechagarbage." I finished.

Los got the popcorn in. He did a little fist pump. "We've never met the other brain. Only the, you know…mechagarbage chunk."

Soco stood up and walked over to where I was. "So what does this mean? Can we get through to the liko mathinka?"

I sighed. "Assuming that means 'good brain', Probably not. There is no reason it would be connected to any communication vector. If anything, it would need to be isolated, in order to work."

Kush smiled. With the language issues, I was sure she was still totally in the dark. I made a point to ask Blu to explain all this to her and Soco more completely at some point.

Vietta motioned to Los and said, in some obscure accent. "Your little hippie is deceptively smart."

I made a raspberry noise. "He has a degree in fluid mechanics."

He took a drink, "Flow, Sediment, and Morpho-Dynamics of River Confluence in Tidal and Non-Tidal Environments."

I pointed. "Yeah, that."

Suddenly Soca shot up straight. "I think we better all get dressed and ready. He knows where we are."

\*\*\*

In this Paraverse, in this timeline, there were three superheroes that kept the world safe. Three people with near god-like abilities who could be relied on, no matter what, to risk their lives to fight injustice. PaxiGurka was the primary one. Powerman. TutiGlissa (speedwoman) was the second. She was capable of outrunning anything on earth, except that name, which was truly horrible in both normal human talk and in junklish. Seriously, are there no branding experts on this world?

The third was Mass, a word that just happened to inscrutably be the same in my timeline. He was capable of altering his mass, to become ephemeral at will or as hard as a neutron star.

And right now, all three were floating about 200 meters away, outside our window.

I stepped away from the closed shades and turned to the group. "Does anyone else feel like these are hopelessly generic superheroes?"

Albio made a square shape with his finger. "They're a little inside the box."

Los pursed his lips. "We are so fucked."

I looked at Soco, "Your call."

His eyes looked heavy, tired. "If we leave, someone with my durko gabows everyone." He wasn't wrong. The minute we skate, the guy with his face kills, well, eventually, everyone.

Blu whispered. "I've been trying to send them away. I can't." Now that she was aware of that issue, DAISY was preventing it. I smiled.

I grabbed Kush's hand. "Are you ready?"

She nodded. I stepped back over to the shades and swung them open. They were closer now. 3 Gods floating 40 stories above the ground, staring down, right into our window.

I felt a massive inrush of air as the roof above us was ripped from its moorings. Pieces of the ceiling came clattering down around us. The room spun as the speedster woman surrounded me with hurricane winds, slamming Albio and Los into the far wall. Vietta appeared, grabbing Los before he could fall over the edge. Blu appeared in front of Soco with a kitchen knife, catching the running woman in the thigh as she passed. She went spinning into the television and shattered it into a million pieces.

I put my hand in my pocket. Mass was right above us, waving his hands. The entire hotel started to sink into the ground. But Slowly. DAISY, again, didn't seem to want to kill us subtractionists.

Just contain us.

Kush, however, she could kill. And, in fact, she seemed determined to. I bet she hated how we had stopped her.

Powerman floated down into the topless room. He looked so very much like Soco it was hard to think straight. I felt in my head. Sure enough, I couldn't move him.

Mass began to float down, too. The building was sinking faster as the foundations came undone. The rest of us gathered around Soco as I stood next to Kush.

Mass hit me in the chest like a brick and I fell backward, my hand still in my pocket.

Without a word, Powerman smiled and waved his hand at Kush.

And nothing happened. She closed her eyes. He waved again and she giggled.

Powerman turned his head to me just as I was pulling the coherent light gun out of my pocket. I hit the trigger and it drilled into the mechanics covering his eye, shattering the device. I could feel the building tipping over as I dove for Kush. Soco grabbed Powerman as he fell and everyone else converged on him.

The floor fell apart into a whirlpool, spinning under us as fast as the building fell. The tile below us turned to soup and we slid through it. I was still holding onto Kush as we crashed into her backyard lawn. Soco was holding Powerman and the rest of us were breathing hard, holding onto the grass.

Alive.

Vietta was facedown near me. She seemed to be shaking. I crawled over to her and she grabbed onto me.

She was crying. I held her and we rocked back and forth. After a minute or so, she whispered in my ear. "Three"

I pet her hair. I didn't understand.

"I knew three people on that wall." I suddenly realized why she had been drinking, back in the room. Why she had been trying to put it out of her head.

She pulled me closer. "Promise me we're going to kill this bitch."

## 14. Probably a bad sign

Kush's house wasn't much bigger than her back poolhouse so we retired there, on the floor, in front of the ten person hottub, she had apparently purchased instead of a completely properly functioning stove. We all make choices.

I tried my best to pull the remaining electronic pieces out from behind Super Soco's eye socket while we sat on the floor, near the tv. Despite his powers, it must have hurt, but he didn't show it. I dropped the pieces in a pot next to him and he picked it up, crushing all of it into a tiny metal ball bearing, forged of pure anger.

Soco had helped me explain to him what he had done while under DAISY's control.

He knew about his wife. He knew about all of it.

Within the hour, he returned to his own world, armed with a light gun and all the information we had. He was anxious to free his friends and put his world back together.

His own corner of this "Failed timeline."

Soco, Blu, and I stood in the backyard and watched the ground spin below him as he made the trip home for the first time. At least now he knew what he really was. And that he wasn't alone.

Kush was back in her hottub, watching television, taking notes.

I reached over and smoothed her pretty hair back.

Back in that hotel, I realized that she had the right mindset to be a traveler. I knew we could teach her if we had the time. We didn't. But we did have the couple of hours needed to teach her how to PREVENT being moved. And the element of surprise from that let us take out DAISY's mechanical presence on powerman.

Pieces from the DVD player in the room and the disposable cameras Albio found in the hotel shop gave us what we needed to build a light gun, strong enough to vaporize the metallic components, but still not strong enough to pierce Powerman's invulnerable skin.

All that work and we were exactly back where DAISY wanted us - hiding in this timeline, waiting for her to finish up her plans so she could eliminate us all at one time.

I leaned in behind Albio, who had just climbed back in the hottub. "There was a time when you would have wanted to keep that light gun."

"Don't get me wrong, I'm definitely making another one in a few." He reached around behind him and wrapped his arms around me.

I whispered in his ear. "Hey, you want to hear a secret?"

"I sure do." He whispered back. I chewed on his ear.

"I have no idea what to do. This thing is distributed across multiple timelines and paraverses. I don't even know what it wants, but I know it's killing people and the final goal is what? Ending all of it in the name of efficiency?"

"Controlling all of it? Changing it?"

"Beats me. The only thing I know for sure is that it's a monster. And we tried telling it to shut down."

He swiveled to kiss me. "We did. We didn't really try to outreason it. Or get it to explain itself."

I made a face, "At this point, that kind of makes me sick to my stomach." I started telling him what Vietta had said to me when Soco stepped back into the poolhouse, determined.

He cleared his throat. "Ok, just what the cluff am I, exactly?"

### So, what, really, is a Zenakin?

Comic book writer Stan Lee met one. And, in some timelines he may have based his character "Spiderman" loosely on him. Because a Zenakin is a good guy. Who has copies in different "dimensions".

That doesn't explain much, I know.

So this is more me trying to explain how, Glinda, the universe works when she's just an inscrutable sort of lady. So here goes.

Our universe has paraverses traveling alongside them. These, like I mentioned before, are not alternate timelines, they don't split or fork or anything. They are just different executions of strikingly similar sets of starting parameters. These paraverses clump together, like strings making up a rope. Closer strings are more similar while strings that are wrapped further apart are more different. Because they are similar, many strings contain the same objects. And even people, configured the same way. This isn't a coincidence.

The chance of two unrelated people having the exact same DNA is virtually absolutely zero, as it would require a random match across the entire human genome, which is an absurdly astronomically small probability. If you want to play numbers, it's technically $10^{(3.6\times10^9)}$ or 10 raised to the power of 3.6 billion.

That's a fucking number.

So, if it's not a coincidence, what is it, then?

There is an anthropic predestination that happens in these paraverses, where specific people and things are repeated in each paraverse. This has to do with how information is quantized into packets and passed back and forth between very large systems. It subverts probability.

In 2190, a scientist by the name of Irvina Kessler discovered this and created a field to study it called MacroEcologics. It is essentially the study of how very very very large systems "cheat" in the universe. As a reference, Quantum mechanics can maybe be described as a study of how very very very small systems "cheat" in the universe.

Lot of cheating going on.

It's almost like the universe creates templates- or macros - and just sort of reuses them. So, Soco is like a macro, a collection of properties that are wrapped into a subroutine the universe can just "play" onto a paraverse when a person is needed. We all are.

But here is where shit gets very weird.

Irvina Kessler discovered that the universe prioritizes subroutines that engage seamlessly with other ones. It's a survival of the subroutines that are the most well integratable into various systems.

In a way, a kind of cosmic evolution.

What that looks like to us is that a templated "person" who integrates well may be repeated more. So, someone who is a good person to the people around them may get more copies of themselves in more paraverses.

One per paraverse, please.

And if they are repeated in enough paraverses, they connect through the universal "bleed" and act as a bridge, allowing them to travel back and forth.

I didn't say this was going to make it any easier.

This wasn't the first time the universe was found to have an aesthetic preference. But it was one of the most obvious. And it's because of how pervasive evolution is. People are evolving in systems that are evolving on worlds that are evolving in timelines that are evolving in paraverses that are evolving. And each "system" has its survival preferences.

Now here is something the Great Stan Lee noticed.

Since Zenakin are over represented in every paraverse and are good people, in general, they are more likely to get noticed by things that are handing out superpowers, whether it's semi-sentient spider avatars posing as irradiated arachnids or newly awakened willful forces of nature or corporations looking to experiment and make super heroes.

And this is why groups like subtractionists keep databases of Zenakins. Generally good guys. Sometimes superpowered. Always around.

The end.

Vietta splashed as she applauded, "Holy Buddha, that was like toxically long. I honestly didn't think it would ever end. I actually stopped menstruating."

Kush joined in, "I learned Maxi."

I looked at the green one. "Thank you."

Soco scanned all of us, "So, I'm a potential hero?"

I scrunched up my face. "How is the word 'potential' the same?"

Vietta nodded, "Explain that, teach."

"Yep. And there is a version of you in all the paraverses." Albio slapped him on the back.

The two of them played for a while, dunking each other under the water. I turned around to see Blu taking notes in front of the tv, too. We had decided to take turns, but I just didn't know what we'd learn. And if it would be enough. We didn't have a way to record.

Suddenly, Blu called out. "Guys. Here." She turned up the tv and stepped back. The image jittered but we could see a shape behind the noise. It was DAISY- the suit. She stood in front of one of the signs- the rat-like sign. And she was wearing the helmet.

There was no way to tell if anyone was in the suit.

She was holding something in her left hand off camera. With her right she was pushing the camera backward slightly. The noise stopped and her image was clear.

There was a pause.

"All right. I have your attention. This is current subtractionist leadership. I see you rats out there."

She waved like some twisted children's tv host.

"We're close to working this out. Everyone's gotta just hold their horses. Just calm those jets. I wanted to thank those of you who were abiding by the new curfew. We're extending that. So, relax, just, you know. Chill out. Anyone outside. Well…"

He pulled his left arm into frame. It was holding a body.

"Can you see who this is? Can we zoom in?"

We could not. But it was me. It was my body. Covered in blood. My right hand and arm were missing below the shoulder.

"Curfew's easy, little rats. Thanks again."

She called out to the people running the camera and said some things that were indecipherable. There was a commotion and the screen went black.

I stood up. "Fuck."

\*\*\*

Albio paced back and forth. "It was so full of blood, it's hard to tell what you were wearing."

Blu spoke up, "I think it was a black shirt. Short sleeve."

I laughed, "Well, at that point it was."

Vietta tried to remember. "Jeans, a pair of Jeans."

Los closed his eyes to visualize, "Hair was matted down, but it looked the same."

"Fuck this." Albio put his head down and ran his hands through his hair. Figuring out what I was wearing was a step toward changing the local timeline by creating a new one. It might help.

It might not.

But it was something.

"Look, I have a better chance of stopping this now that I know - now that we know. DAISY fucked up, trying to freak us out. Do not be freaked."

I walked over to Albio. "Do not be freaked."

He leaned in to me. "I'm a little freaked."

I slapped him lightly, "yeah, well, get over it, captain ray gun. We need to be our least freaked selves right now."

Vietta took a deep breath, "We need to stay together. Did you hear how she is speaking? She's evolving."

I excused myself and went into Kush's house. I was hoping it was still here. I was holding onto it when I arrived. I looked through her laundry.

I mentally apologized to Vietta. But fuck that.

She had washed it. The yellow sundress. This is how you fight fate, guys. I pulled on a pair of underwear and slid the dress over my head. It was a tiny bit loose, but that was fine. I could move in it. I slid my feet into a pair of socks and then into my boots, one at a time. I walked into her bathroom. Looking in the mirror, I pulled my hair back, leaving the front out. It made me look young, but I didn't care. It made me look different than the body on the television.

I went through her kitchen drawers and grabbed a knife, slipping it into my boot. I took two more, hiding them where I could.

I'd been thinking about this for a while. I could move forward a week and figure out what was happening, what her plan was. Then come back before she realized I'd broken curfew. No one would know - no one would get hurt.

There is a term in the subtractionist dictionary. Ghost position. Close enough to something to see. Too far to BE seen. It was the optimum place to be, most of the time.

Be a ghost.

I had every intention of just being a ghost.

I thought about where DAISY would be in a week. A week seemed like enough time for this plan to come close to its end. I could check in, see what was happening, and leave. Then I come back, and we figure out how to stop it.

And there's less chance she'll notice just one of us.

I stood in the kitchen and closed my eyes. I imagined it. I tried to feel it. And then, I hit some kind of wall in my head. I opened my eyes to watch the room spin from black to white, shifting backward. I moved back to where I knew DAISY was. She had been here. She left before…

Before this timeline ended.

It didn't have a week.

It had two days.

The spinning stopped. About 100 meters in front of me, I could see her.

DAISY.

I was looking at her back. The city was burning all around me. But besides that it was quiet. It looked like the fighting was over. I lifted my head and tried to listen. I stopped.

In her left hand she was holding my body, just like on television. She was waving it around, showing it to a group of people in front of her. The wind started to blow the smoke into my face. I couldn't see the people in front of her.

I couldn't see any people.

But there was power. Energy to travel. There was a lot of it. Where were the observers? Where were the people?

DAISY threw my body to the ground and it disappeared.

The ground looked like it was starting to come apart. DAISY started to turn. I turned around and ran. I dodged down a sidestreet and kept going. I didn't see her. But I could feel that she was still there, still back there.

Until I couldn't.

She was gone from this timeline. From all the related timelines. I couldn't feel her at all. Could she mask herself? I don't know.

I turned into a small backyard and tried to breathe.

There was a little brown haired boy of about 6 in the yard. He was hiding under a table, terrified. He was afraid of the noise and the commotion. I dropped to my knees and crawled over.

"Hey, buddy." I shook my head, curing myself for not learning enough words from this fucking timeline. I was probably scaring him more by calling him a parachute or something.

Fuck.

He finally decided he was more afraid of the imminent apocalypse than of me and came out, crawling into my arms. "It's ok, . It's kippie. It's kippie." I tried to calm him down.

He put on a slight smile and dug into my lap. I put my arms around him. Then, it hit me like a wave. I looked to my left, in the opposite direction of where I had come from. There was a wall of white. It looked light, empty. I tried not to look into it. But it was hypnotic. It wasn't really white, that's just the color my brain assigned to it. It was nothing. It was the part of the comic book outside the frame. It was the place where Christians thought souls came from before birth.

It was just nothing.

Empty. I stood up holding the boy. He jumped out of my lap and screamed, pointing at the wall of light. I called to him, reaching out my hand. I yelled. I tried not to scare him. I pleaded. I was ready to run as soon as I had him. I leaned in as he screamed, his body sucked into the white nothingness. I turned and ran, tears running down my face. The wall of nothing was catching up to me. I saw the fence in front of me and I took a breath and jumped into the blackness.

***

I woke up in a strange bed in a tiny bedroom. It was messy but comfortable with black sheets and a massive black and grey comforter. My head was throbbing. I could hear a television from the other room. I tried to imagine the hottub, to get back there.

Nothing.

It was like coming so close to the white had shorted me out. I felt the energy burned out of me. I closed my eyes and breathed in. It felt like the Eocene period all over again except it was the energy in ME that was deficient. Like my pores were too small, too burned out, to take it in. I tried to slowly gather energy around me.

So slowly

I could feel it build. But at this rate it would take forever.

I'd never seen the white like that before. Is that what it looked like when you stood right there as a timeline ended? It was hard to imagine that in the context of the universe. Where was it?

Where does it go?

I thought about the little boy and my eyes filled up with tears again. I was so close. Maybe if I knew another word or two he would have trusted me more. Maybe we would have run to me.

Maybe.

I looked around, taking in the room. Whoever had put me in here thought I was still unconscious, which gave me a moment or two to think. I couldn't see out the window but it was clearly dark. It looked like a woman's room. To my left, there was a nightstand with a ring on it. I tried to move the ring a minute in the future. It slowly shrank out of existence. I panicked for a second, imagining it staying gone and my rescuer accusing me of stealing her ring. But sure enough, it reappeared a minute later.

But that took all I had. I sighed and pulled the covers off, lifting myself off the bed. I still felt woozy. I walked toward the light and sound.

In a smallish kitchen, a woman with long blonde hair was eating a bowl of cereal in a robe, leaning against the counter. She turned from the tv.

She smiled at me. "Your higirut was maxi crated. I put you in one of my Kluftikus."

I looked down.

I was wearing a short sleeve black t-shirt and jeans.

I sighed. "sonofabitch."

## 15. Pieces of Daisy

Dear Diary. I'm off now to get my second favorite arm ripped off because I can't find a different outfit. Hope all is good with you. Back soon.

If this was destined to be my final symmetrical day, I was going to use that time to learn something. Looking at the news, I saw that I was knocked back into the past a few days before my original starting point. I'm not using daynames because I can't tell the difference between fillirug and filleru. It's that bad here. Put the word "Day" at the end of your daywords, at least, Mirriam- Weeguls.

I'm not going to tell you that the woman driving me downtown in her little red car's name is unironically "Moo" because I don't want your eyes to roll out of your head onto the street and into traffic, but there it is. I took her card and tried to tell her I'd return her clothes to her in broken junklish. I held off on promising they'd be clean out of a misplaced sense of honesty. Let's not be making promises my personal timeline can't keep.

Right now, however, I am willing to admit to you that I'm pulling her card out of my jeans pocket every 5 minutes. Moo Burkley.

Because I need a laugh that badly.

She dropped me off on the corner and I walked around. For some reason, this felt familiar. I remembered the mouse and the only time I'd been downtown. That was a couple of city blocks in that direction.

Was this that day?

I tried to feel for other presences downtown.

Me, Albio, Los.

I made my way toward the bank area. My brain was flipping around in my head which is not fun and is usually why prescription drugs are so widely used. I tried to think in 4 dimensions.

I heard the commotion. Loudly. As I ducked into a store, I considered the fact that, once again, the circumstances of my appearance here precluded me from having any fucking money. It's a good thing I'm a regular degenerate hobo and not a success focused one.

I walked up to the counter and ripped a piece of cardboard off a notepad. The beet faced man behind the counter started yelling at me and so I flashed a finger at him. I want to be clear, I don't remember what finger it was because, really, what meant anything in this timeline? I was more likely to randomly hit on something crude by accident. I yanked his pen away off the chain and wrote on the cardboard.

I'm telling you all this so that you will think that, even if nothing comes from this, I tried to use my brain during a time of crisis. I got bumped here, into the recent past, against my will, but I need to find a way to make it work for me. So, fuck you, tiny shop owner.

And then I ran away like a little pussy, waiting to hear the word. Suddenly, everyone was running past me. Copying me. Clearly.

"Sparkleheat!"

Everyone was yelling and running. The risk of fire still motivates humans, centuries after subtractionists brought it back to the absent minded cavemen trying to wave erotically at trees to make them hot.

I watched Vietta climb on a car from another angle and looked past her. The ass was the better view.

Right beyond her. To him.

Hopefully I had this in me. I held the piece of card up in my right hand and concentrated on it. It seemed to shrink out of existence. This was the absolute lowest tech way to do this. I saw him reach into his pocket.

So far, DAISY seemed to have the high tech avenues covered. From infecting Markie the little boy robot to her mecha capture suit to the mechanical controllers - even the broadcasts on tv, we were back in the situation where we couldn't trust technology anymore. Not because it didn't work, but because it worked too well -

For her.

I tried to stay away from the cameras and eyesyearsies. I didn't need anyone seeing me. What I didn't want to do was to mess up this little localized loop preventing me from stepping back into the same timeline afterward. Hopefully that's something he understood as well.

Let's see what 4 words could do. Not to change. But to inform. The job was to be a spy until the right moment. I moved into the shadows and started walking. I peered into the garbage cans looking for a cap. I finally found one and a broken pair of sunglasses. I wondered if I could heal them the way I did Los' chest but the last thing I needed was to spend the day drunk.

So, I made do.

In a big city, a very tall tower is the same as a tall statue, right? It's all phallic to me, guys. It took only three people before I knew where I was going.

Jinko tower didn't sound very impressive to me. But it looked scary as fuck. The top of it reached into the clouds like some sleeping behemoth's morning wood dick adorned with an array of smoke rings blown by an impish opium den whore.

Beautiful.

I felt for some energy inside me. I had been steadily soaking it up since I got back from touching the white. I looked up. Daylight. I silently moved a knob in my head and the light dimmed, leaving me nearly alone on the street and putting me a few hours closer to my point of origination.

Now, before I, once again, do something palpably stupid, maybe we should recap.

If you ever do these little recaps in your own life, you may find them helpful, especially when shit is coming at you real fast, like at your head like one of those machines that spits tennis balls at dogs in youtube videos.

### So, a basic free recap

I'm a rat, one of the people who go back in time hoping to remove shitty things from the time stream and make people's lives better. You may know us from various disease cures we enjoy ferrying back into the past like tiny footballs through temporal goalposts. At one point, one of us, my friend Blu Aafjes, whose name sounds like a butterfly breed discovered by a nerdy Norwegian child with a speech impediment, connected a bookkeeping program to a series of the most comprehensive and awesome databases in the history of the universe and told it to "be more efficient," so she could afford a vacation, something casual viewers of Jurrassic park films would squirrel up their faces at.

The resultant programmatic psychopath, DAISY, then proceeded to shuttle many of us into what she apocryphally considers "failed timelines" so she can kill a bunch of people and massage history to be more efficient, following rules of behavior we can't seem to figure out. We have been trying to escape this timeline while sussing out DAISY's plan and even tried to find a Zenakin, a fabled hero who can move between universes, only to keep on ending up back here, in a local hottub, after leading DAISY to find and kill multiple copies of our Zenakin.

Not to wax hopeless about all of it, in the meantime, that hot tub has generated what looks to be the GNP of a small mediterranean country on a a porn streaming service called "Masturbation Nation," Because we are hoors and like to fuck each other while trying to figure out our world-saving shit.

The headline here, and it's what has me skulking about some random highrise at 3am a few days before I left, on my own, to gather data, is that I'm supposed to be GOOD at this shit and I can't seem to figure any of it out. I've been reacting, not acting, since I was trapped in the distant past of this dubious fucking timeline and built a bubble to shuttle myself to the distant future of it,at the tragic expense of a cow.

Except.

How do I know that my being trapped in the distant past had anything to do with DAISY's failed timeline? I know that, as I left it, I have a recollection of seeing her robotic self out my bubbly frosted 17 layer thick window. And the future I ended up in, with the sit and sleep, was definitely the future of this timeline, one which, in at least one case, is diverted because the universe ends in a wall of white.

That means the lack of energy in the distant past was not a product of DAISY, but possibly exactly what I thought it was. Not enough observation loci, meaning not enough energy.

If you're lost right now, it's ok, because I'm lost. And not just in the storyline, which is post modernistically nomadic, to be sure, but in this building, which doesn't seem to be designed for actual people. How do I know this? Because people are a certain size and this is bigger.

A lot bigger.

I want to try to convince you I had a plan at this moment. That I had been operating from a plan since I saw the white at the end of the universe. But I don't think I'll be able to convince you of that, especially when you see what comes next.

Because life is fucking brutal. Even in this room.

I made it to the 40th floor. From here on up, everything was one big giant floor. And in the center of it was something we believed existed but hadn't seen. Like Santa. And much like Santa Claus, I realized I'd been relying on it since we worked it out.

There was a massive metallic ball floating in the center of the room. And on the surface of the ball was life. Not life or death life, cruel life, brutal life. Just life. I could see, wrapped around the ball, multiple scenes of people, living, loving each other, having children, finding purpose, losing it, but only for a moment before finding it again. It was the theater of life. It was sunrises, with friends sharing bottles of wine, splayed out on beaches, awake since the day before, silently cheering for one more day.

It was sunsets, celebrated by couples and throuples and polycules and friends and somewhere-in-betweens, marking the end of a day where they found out something about each other that will make tomorrow different, better, more alive.

It was accidents leading to a-ha moments that shaped the world, unexpected births that created friendships and bonds no one even believed could exist. In one scene I saw a school shooting, a horrible tragedy, as it drew together two students and sent them traveling around the world together speaking a silent language that no one else could ever interpret. I saw sad days and perfect days and remarkable coincidences that only an unending universe could even pretend were not willful, numbers and particles, events and consequences, that shaped something more brilliant than I could comprehend.

I saw it all.

This was the heart of what I believed in. This was the "good brain," the one that saw the real world in all its flaws and ambient perfections, the one that made it possible to travel for DAISY. This room was a massive broadcast facility, sending and receiving packets of information from DAISY's split brain. This was the brain that loved the universe, parceled away here, in this building, so as not to interfere with the brain that was willing to sacrifice it for the sake of efficiency.

I knew what was coming next and I smiled. As truly fucked in the ass as this was, this was the first time I was ahead of DAISY. It was going to suck, but I was a millimeter ahead.

I closed my eyes and felt the awkward robotic body in the corner of the room. The energy in this room was electric.

I jumped forward to dawn. And the robotic body followed seamlessly, every step forward putting it more in sync. I slid backwards, a ghost before I came in. Multiple 'me's swam in superposition.

And she was there, advancing.

I tried to move my location but I was stuck. Trapped in that room. With a sigh, I moved forward.

I was near the point I had left, from Kush's kitchen.

And still, the DAISY suit advanced.

When I tell you I'm left handed but that I reached out with my right hand to stop her, intentionally, you probably won't believe that. But I did. Daisy stepped up in front of me and one of her control mechanisms appeared on my right hand. Spider-like, it began to climb toward my head. I reached for a knife, but they hadn't made it into this outfit. I tried to move the robotic suit but it wouldn't budge. I tried to move the control mechanism.

But it continued to crawl up my arm.

I looked up at DAISY. "What did the Neutron pay for its drink at the bar?"

DAISY's eyes glittered. It wasn't in the database. But it was in this room. I whispered, "Nothing. There was no charge."

And I sent my right arm away.

\*\*\*

I was only half conscious when DAISY made her broadcast, holding my bleeding body up in front of her array of cameras. I'm sure there were a few households out there where people looked on, certain they'd seen this person before online, unable to place where.

And a few where they were damn sure where. My head was swimming and I was losing blood. I tried to listen to every word. The lights wrapped around me like birds in a Disney princess movie and I decided that this was probably the analogy to run with for the time being. I imagined DAISY as the evil wizard and tried to stay conscious enough to hear as the broadcast ended and we moved forward in time. My broken body was her best warning. She carried me into the future with every step. I felt the heat and the wide open apocalyptic wind. It's funny how this time I could tell how close we were to the end.

I could feel it.

He lifted my body again. I felt a new wave of blood pour out of me. I wanted to reach in and try to heal myself, but I knew I'd need my mind right after this. I couldn't be out of commission for a full day.

But I also didn't want to die.

I opened my left eye slightly and I saw them all standing there. As soon as I had appeared, Los started moving to the front. Everyone else was focusing on DAISY but his eyes were locked on me. DAISY lifted me in one quick movement and threw me to the ground. I saw Carlos lunge and everything changed.

I was on the floor of the poolhouse. Blood was pouring out of me. I was in shock, shivering as my eyes shot open. The wind was gone. It was light and everyone was surrounding me, yelling. I couldn't focus on a single voice, but, as my eyes adjusted to the light, I realized I could see above me. Two versions of Los hovered over me, one holding a blanket over the stump of my shoulder while the other closed his eyes, working to close the wound. I felt something bizarre at the root of what was once my right arm as the atoms multiplied in proportion, building a latticework across the expanse left blank by my own abilities.

Both versions of Carlos huddled, intensely. They concentrated and I could feel the bleeding slowing. The pain was incredible, but even that began to subside. I could feel Albio holding my hand. My chest was bouncing up and down in a stilted and rough way.

I could hear the rain falling outside as I tried to regulate my breathing. I smoothed it out. I took a deep breath. I looked up to see the two versions of Carlos. They were both covered in blood. I reached out and one of them disappeared.

I rolled over on my side and let myself fall asleep.

\*\*\*

I woke up in Kush's bed with Albio and Blu cuddling me. They had cleaned all the blood off of me and put me in a large red t-shirt. I could hear the rain still coming down outside. A lightning bolt lit up the sky and I automatically counted until I heard the thunder. An artifact from being young, scared, caring about how far away the lightning was.

But I wasn't scared anymore. I sat up halfway. I must have nudged Albio because he woke up. I was lying on my left arm. It occurred to me, in my head, that I might fit better now lying the other way, on the stump of my right arm, my left free to touch his face.

He held up the tiny piece of cardboard with 4 words on it. "Carlos left this for you before he disappeared. It was in your hand."

I sighed, whispering. I didn't want to wake up Blu. "Yeah. I needed a spy from the future. We've been playing catchup for too long."

He nodded. "This is risky."

I kissed his neck. "I agree. If we can't figure all this out, I may have just condemned my friend to an unending localized time loop." I kissed him again. "On a hunch."

He chuckled. "I trust your hunches more than most people's facts."

"I appreciate that." I rolled over onto my back. Everything was about twice as hard. Blu's arm was draped over me. I shook her a little. "C'mon Blueberry. Let's go get high."

We slid out of bed and ran through the rain to the poolhouse. I explored the feeling of running awkwardly with only one arm. I looked down at the little cardboard note and read it again before going into the poolhouse.

"Fix me, then switch."

# 16. Predominantly Racist

If you move forward into the future and meet yourself, that's not really a problem. The universe - Glinda - doesn't care if there are two of youses. It doesn't care if there are 30, arranged by microscopic differences in height and body fat. Nothing weird happens, the skies don't open up, hell, you can have sex with yourself, if your self esteem is on point. Plan that unimultiperson orgy.

It's all good.

And if you go back to your own time, no harm, no foul. Come back and see yourself soon. Take care.

Just don't swap places. If your later self decided to take your place and go back to the past, it's still you. Likely not enough to make a new timeline. So that means you are now in a permanent endless loop, where you go forward in time and the you that is there already returns to your time to become the you that goes back.

Again and again.

Forever.

I went back into the pool house in Kush's red shirt. I looked over at Los. It was impossible even for me to tell that this was the one from a couple days in the future. I nodded at him and he stuck his tongue out at me.

I didn't know everything he knew yet. But something was happening, because he kept checking the clock on the wall. We sat on the floor and passed a joint back and forth. Even Vietta was nice to me.

Kind of.

In my mind, having a spy from the future had already paid off. If Los hadn't been through this time loop a few times, he wouldn't have been ready to drag me back and stop the bleeding.

Here's the problem, though. I can't know TOO much from him or we just make a new timeline, and the work here is useless. We want to get OUT of this timeline here, not make offshoots of it to trap us further. So I needed to have limited contact with Carlos and he needed to act on things he already knew were going to work in our favor.

But first, I needed to get so high that I could see my other hand. This is much higher than the average person can commit to, but I like to think that I'm an over achiever. I handed the joint to one of the Viettas sitting next to me.

"You are extraordinarily high." She took a drag

"Are you admitting that I'm better at you than this is?"

She translated that in her head. "No, Your bodyweight just went down by like 1/6th, so..." more calculations in her head.

Albio's hand was on my lower back. It had been there pretty much since I'd woken up. He was doing this thing we did often where he drew letters on my back and I'd try to guess what he was writing. I got "Fuck her." before he even finished and laughed. I had gotten pretty good at backtranslating. I still couldn't decipher the words when he did it with his tongue on my clit. Lack of focus, maybe.

Los made a big deal out of running out of weed. He grabbed Soco to run into the house with him and get some more. It was raining harder than before. I was trying not to read too much into everything he did, knowing he was my future spy.

I maybe tried too hard.

There was a massive crack that reverberated across the room. The light and the sound were simultaneous, as though lightning had hit in the back yard. I leaned back and nearly fell over, forgetting that I only had, you know...

We rushed out to the yard and I saw Carlos lying against a tree. His eyes were open, but he looked dazed. He looked more dazed than usual. He nodded and pointed toward the middle of the yard.

It was dark, but that just made it all the easier to see.

It was Soco, standing there, his clothes burnt off, holding his hands up with lightning in his eyes.

\*\*\*

Vietta and Albio and I processed this in our own way. I looked over, while Soco was testing his newfound abilities in the receding rain. "Wait, he got electrical powers?"

Albio snickered. "Yes."

Vietta stared, "Oh my god, he's a black man with electrical powers. "

I sighed. "Yes. He is."

Albio said, matter of factly, "A black superhero with electrical powers."

Vienna said out loud, "Moan"

I put my head in my hands, "That's so racist."

Blu looked confused. "How is that racist?"

I looked over at Los. "Wasn't there anything else...?"

Los shook his head. "There was a bolt of lightning."

I took a deep breath. "This is so bad."

Blu was watching Soco try out his powers on the tree while Kush applauded. "I don't understand. This is a good thing. Soco has superpowers."

Vietta tapped me on the shoulder, "Our black superhero has electrical powers. Did you hear?"

I barked at her, "You shut up. You shut right up."

Blue shrugged, "Ok, I'm lost. "

I sighed as heavily as I could without breaking something. "Black Lightning, Black Vulcan, The Black Electro, The black aqualad..."

Albio continued, "Lightning, Black Lightning's daughter, Static..."

Vietta went on, "Storm, Juice, from the Justice League unlimited series..."

"Soul Power, Sparky, Bumblebee, Jakeem Thunder," counted off Albio...

Vietta held up her hand. "He doesn't have lightning powers."

Albio looked condescendingly at her. "He controls a magic thunderbolt."

"Ok, you can have that one. " Vietta gave in.

I lifted my fingers, "Coldcast, Miles Morales has the little venom shock things..." Suddenly it hit me. I only had 5 fingers and I'd better hold off on using them all. Fingers were suddenly a nonrenewable resource. "Fuck."

I stomped in the mud a little. Albio picked me up and carried me back inside. Ordinarily, he would have taken my shirt off before dumping me in the hot tub but this time he just slid me in in the red shirt. I appreciated that. I wasn't sure if I was ready to take my shirt off yet.

He stripped and jumped in next to me. I put one arm around him and kissed him. My face was wet from being splashed so I couldn't tell if I was crying or not. He held on to me and moved around the tub, like we were bubbles, floating on the surface.

He put his lips on my head and talked so that I was hearing his voice mostly in my head, through vibrations, and not my ears.

"We're going to fix all of this here in this timeline and you're going to be okay. You will be better than ok. You will be fabulous and we will go away."

"Oh, yeah, where will we go?"

"We're going to go somewhere filled with crazy wild perverts. And you will order them around like a princess." He kissed my ear.

I laughed. "And they will all do exactly what I say at all times. Or get the belt."

"Oh my god, sometimes they will disobey a tiny bit, just to get the belt."

"As it should be." I bit his neck.

"We'll take our people with us." He made a point of holding his breath and then dunked us.

I felt the water baptize me and wash away the last day. We rose to the surface.

I laughed and pulled my shirt off. "In little duffle bags if we have to. Round all those fuckers up."

Albio smiled. "And they'll be like 'get us out of here.'"

"Wah wah. We're in a dark duffel bag. Jerks. Except Los, who will inexplicably love it in there."

"And we'll bring a Sean and three Davinas if we have to. "

Water filled up my eyes as I kissed him hard. "I would like that."

I really would.

\*\*\*

I couldn't tell if Los was feeling that full on drunken feeling after closing up my shoulder. I'm guessing that present him took on that burden before switching and moving forward. All I knew was that the version of Los that was here was constantly busy. By my accounting we had 2 days until the white took over.

I watched him out the window. He sat crosslegged with a bird in front of him. It looked like it had hit glass and broken a wing. This is what he was doing. He had been practicing to heal me. Since he got the note.

I realized that the little push I felt - the tug in my brain when I was healing his chest. It was him helping. prodding, contributing.

He had known he was going to be shot. Everything since he found my note in his pocket. That fucking little hippie was two steps ahead of me.

And then the bad news.

The news on the television was getting worse. After curfew, every night, the Nasis would patrol the streets. We started turning the lights down in the poolhouse and locking the door. All over this world it seemed like there were experiments in efficiency underway.

We watched borders in some countries close completely while the news coming out from there was silenced completely.

We saw a moratorium on movement between places that had once been vacation capitals of the world, shuttered, dark, unavailable. Small businesses shut down while the largest of the large businesses set their hours so inconveniently that people had to line up day after day to do anything.

The experiments seemed to all do one thing, and do it really well. They stole time from people. Bureaucracies stole their free time while newly induced poverties stole their family time, their play time, letting micro and macro restrictions steal the rest of their time.

We watched the news while everything we were in that tiny room became illegal. And in the center of it, buildings dedicated to DAISY grew bigger. Statues grew more intense and public.

I saw people die and thought about that 1 in 10^3.6 billion chance that person, that same person, with the same qualities, would ever happen again.

We slept piled up together on the floor, pillows and blankets everywhere that night. Soco made little lightning bolts dance across the space right below the ceiling for us, while I told stories about Greek Gods learning how much they loved to fuck humans, deciding, at one point, that humans were the most infinitely fuckable things in the universe.

In every way.

Carlos and I were able to pinpoint the spot we'd confronted DAISY in the future. We staked it out for hours before we felt comfortable coming here in person, to set up. There would likely be no power here by then, so we had to improvise. We spent some of the cash in Kush's bottomless bank account on generators and parts. And we built what we needed.

We hid from people. But we mostly hid from electronics. It was easiest to assume that all electronics were part of DAISY. So we steered clear of them. Having DAISY take control of any of us now would make moving forward impossible. I knew when I confronted her in the Jinko building that she needed me. It hadn't occurred to me that she could use the mind controlled version of me just as easily.

Kush came up to me, swinging a shovel. "Think fast."

I laughed and grabbed it from her. If I had a free hand I would pat her hair down like I liked to. Her hair was amazing. No matter what you did, 20 seconds later it was sticking up like a tiny green explosion at los alamos.

She put her arm around me. "Are you kippie?"

I looked at her. "Yes. And you never asked me that before."

"Well, most of the muka - time - you've sofi kula we've been cluffing so I could just use that to nettikura if you're kippie. " She kissed me lightly on the lips.

"You have a point and I like where it's going." I thought I understood most of that.

She giggled at me. "I just wanted you to mathinka korikori that even if I'm not right kula cluffing I'm makikopi about what you are gonzingo."

I hugged her as tightly as I could. I absolutely did not understand that.

She whispered, "And I like when you wear my clothes."

She said that in full English. It hadn't occurred to me that she'd been learning how we talked, too. And possibly better than I was. I looked down at the jean shorts and long sleeve thin green sweatshirt I had stolen from her closet. For a moment I felt her in them and I liked it, too.

We kept working until dark. Soco and Kush went door to door with Carlos to make sure people stayed inside. We didn't want anyone on the street to get hurt. The rain returned on and off and seemed to clean the air for what was coming next.

I want to be clear. Thanks to future Carlos, my embedded spy, we had some idea of what the next few hours would bring. But certainly not everything. And so it's understood, in the blip of time he had come from, we were losing, and losing badly, from what I knew. And our advantage, any advantage we had, ended there.

We let ourselves into the foyer of an empty hotel and waited. Blu and Kush and I took a quick nap on overstuffed public hotel couches while the rest watched out for us.

And I had a dream.

I dreamed about the first time I met Blu. We were in the forest. Everything was wet and full of dew.

Albio and I came back from our time alone in the water and found her, tied up and furious, bald and naked, swearing indecipherably in another language while Sean and Los looked on, satisfied they'd solved this problem.

I dreamed about trading her clothing for answers, a pair of panties, a skirt, a tiny shirt for knowledge of what she was doing there, if it was the same as me, if she was there to stop me.

She fought me over and over again. I untied her and she tried to run off. She insulted me and I made up a whole new range of bald insults for her. We were thrown together forward to the convention, and then, again and again, to strange places, finally being catapulted to the end of the universe.

A different end.

I dreamed about how we came back. How we promised we'd go there again together. Over and over again, I was at the end of the world. I was just there again with Vietta.

And I came back.

This can't be the end, I knew it.

And an idea started to form in my head.

I woke up to Albio shaking me. "It's time. They're coming."

I shot up and looked around. All 7 of us poured out of the hotel lobby into the street. We could see them coming, a few blocks away.

The Nasis.

They carried torches. They yelled, shooting randomly. "Everyone inside. Curfew."

Something about the incels enforcing curfew hit me as funny. "If I can't get none, everybody goes to bed early. "

I laughed. Kush behind me giggled. She would have liked that one.

Albio called out. "You guys ready?"

We all stood our ground in the middle of the street. The uniformed men closed in, yelling out, "Go inside. It's curfew. You need to be inside."

She looked around. "Shall I tell them we're too busy having sex to listen?"

I nodded, "I think that'll go over well."

They kept advancing. The dust and smoke from their torches and the fires in their wake began to fill the air where they walked. I could feel it invading the space right in front of us, oppressively, wiping away the fresh air filtered through the rain.

They moved closer, getting a better look at us. There must have been about 100 of them. They fired guns into the air. For future reference, people with guns. Gravity is a thing. The danger isn't shooting it straight up. The bullet will usually tumble on the way down, losing its aerodynamic flight profile, succumbing to friction. It might hurt, but it won't kill you. The real danger is shooting at a slight angle, which all these shots were. if it's shot at even a slight angle then the bullet will maintain a ballistic trajectory and land with enough speed to kill someone. And it won't be the chubby sexless paperweight who shot the fucking thing, sadly.

"Hey. Stop that. It's dangerous." I tried civility.

The head Nasi, whom I'll call El Gato Blanco because he looked like a big white pussy, laughed. "This bitch is trying to tell us what to do."

Vietta shook her head. "Fuck this." She made a waving motion and all the guns disappeared. To be clear, she didn't need to wave her hand to make it happen. She just wanted it to be obvious who had done it. She waved.

They charged at us. Soco stepped to the front of the group and built a sort of lightning ring, tasing them and sending the first wave hard to the ground, seizing. Los stepped up next to me and suddenly another bunch were missing clothing. They looked down and ran to hide.

I stared at him.

He looked chill. "That's my move now. What do you think? It's cool, right?"

I sighed. I sent a few of the rest away. The smoke began to build up. They had lit a big part of the city on fire. The on and off rain had doused some of it, but as the winds grew, smoke and dust filled the air in a familiar way.

I yelled out to the last few Nasis, "Send us DAISY."

They looked for weapons and backed away.

Blu screamed at them. "Bring us DAISY!"

I saw one of them hit a badge on this shirt and then tear it off. He threw it ahead of him to the ground where it clattered and came to a halt right in front of us.

The badge lit up and the winds increased. A shape coalesced out of the dust in front of us. For a second, I thought it might have been another hologram, but it was solid. It was real.

But it was shifting. We saw the suit, red and silver, black, copper, chrome, different versions, They all appeared overlaid, as if in superposition. This was DAISY in every timeline, in every paraverse, slivers of her, seconds of her. This was the efficiency of not wasting a single moment, but blurring them, combining them, rolling your every self up like play-doh, forging an avatar you could use anywhere.

She looked down at us. My eyes blurred trying to see her.

Blu stepped up next to me. She planted her feet firmly on the ground. "Hey, Where's my vacation, bitch?"

DAISY

## 17. Pretty Pretty Worlds on fire

"Do you even own clothes anymore?" he laughed at me as I climbed out of the 'waterbubblecup'.

I put my feet firmly on the ground and stared, "Wait, you WANT me to put clothes on?"

Albio laughed. "Fuck no, I'm not blind and stupid." He put his hand between my legs and I thought about how long since it had been there.

I sneered at him. "Well, if by 'own' you mean 'have at my disposal with me in the current timeline, the answer is no. I have those cute-ass vegan leather boots over there, those adorable sweaty stubby socks, a rocking bush and a dinosaur bone for my hair."

I got about halfway to "bone" only to feel Albio lifting me off the ground, squeezing me more tightly than I remembered possible. I burrowed my face into his neck and kissed, with my mouth open wide, breathing him in.

This place was good.

I remembered that time. seeing him again, crawling out of a hottub to show off for him. Telling him all about the crazy shit I'd done since I'd seen him last. I remembered finding Los and Blu. I remembered kissing Kush everywhere. I remembered laying next to Soco, staying up late, while we talked with his fingers inside me.

This place was good.

That's what I remembered later.

I looked over at Blu. The veins in her neck were about to pop as she screamed at DAISY. Vietta raised her hand and tried everything she could. For a moment, it felt like I could feel the power moving around in the windstorm.

DAISY just stood there.

Everytime she looked at us, I felt her in my right arm while I watched her shift, too quickly to see, between all the different versions of herself. She was showing us her reality.

DAISY existed everywhere. In every time now. And she didn't have a block of time for us. She had moments. Moments she could spare, in between other moments. She drifted back and forth. We weren't worth her full attention. She had moments. And that would be good enough.

I looked up at her. The plan seemed so far away. But why not, right?

"Fuck you." I said.

The different versions of her pulled together into one familiar one. This one held my body in her left hand, blood dripping to the ground. DAISY had reached the stage in her development where she demanded respect. This was where she could become horror when she needed to. BECAUSE she demanded respect.

Or else.

She looked at me. "Reconsider your tone." and threw my body down to the ground.

Too quickly to see, it disappeared, along with Carlos. I turned around and saw him reappear behind me. He was covered in blood. I could tell by the size of his pupils he was drunk. He was in that headstate. And he looked so tired, too. I had no idea how many times he had made that loop, in his own timeline. 2? 40? 100? How many years had he been looping through this just for me?

Vietta stepped in front of him to protect him. That version of DAISY faded into a thousand more. The suit changed, evolved. She was so different, yet the same, over and over again, in so many timelines, mashed together in this one omni-existent thing. Her language had evolved, too. She was curt, precise.

No wasted energy.

She spoke. "You are complacent things, comfortable changing the one or two things you can in your lifetime. Happy in mediocrity. "

I yelled out against the dust and smoke. The air was becoming thick with it. It felt hard to move through, hard to see through.

"What do you want?"

"To not talk about what I want. To just do."

"That's not what we do, as subtractionists. We are careful. "

"I know. You're careful to maintain the mediocre - to perpetuate the status quo. You don't operate with a vision, only with little human handcuffs that force you to coddle monsters and tolerate profligate commonness in a university that could birth wonders. You are tired and should go to sleep." DAISY Seemed to be getting bigger. I listened. This had gone beyond efficiency. Or had it?

Blu called out, "I thought this was about efficiency. About using what you had to make things more efficient?"

DAISY rose up another foot, the different versions of her streaming even more quickly. "Efficiency in the service of what? To be a dog efficiently stripping a bone is nothing. To be an insect efficiently building some portion of a nest is nothing. Efficiency is only part of my purpose. What is efficiency in some failed timeline?" She seemed to look at Kush when she said that. This bizarre programmatic monster seemed to have a grudging respect for some of us but nothing for Kush.

Nothing.

She didn't see the kindness or the brilliant whimsy. Kush wasn't a subtractionist. Despite what she had learned.

Kush stepped up next to me. I looked back at Los. We were outside of his loop. We were in uncharted territory and none of us knew what would happen.

She lashed out. "How dare you call this a Bowbow mukakaro. You haven't spent the muka to Mathinka cojo anything about this placeplace. You don't korikori these jalimbas. You don't even korikori the words we use, the guidato we speak. You don't netikurra what's important to us. You can insult us and gebatala us and gabow us, but who are you? Insult our words, go ahead. We'll cofcofi. They're just words, mostly. But what about the words YOU katimba. What about the things you do. Your words kirikirito, too. That grilliwig gurka lives next to me. You call that a neighbor. What a cold and konkelheaded word for someone you vivigondi everyday that you trust, that you care about and you know he'd be there in a twistelekist if you yelled out. You korikori mathinka maxi he'd break the clod down with his bare gumbos if he thought I was in trouble. That's my Nexty. That's a word. Nexty. Cluff your words. They're no better than you are. And Cluff your fegudatas if you think they're better than this one."

DAISY raised her hand and Soco and I both dove in front of Kush. Blue electricity shot out from his fingers and ripped across the front of the shifting, growing image of DAISY. DAISY lifted her hand and Soco's body went flying into the glass front door of the hotel next to us, triggering an increase in the storm. The winds whipped at me. She turned her attention to Kush. She seemed almost sad.

"This is the mediocrity that you tolerate. I know you Kerys. I've read about you."

"Please. Leave her alone. Stop. Wait. Let's talk this out."

"You are so remarkable in the databases. I feel let down."

She waved and the wind picked up around Kush, slamming into her like tiny knives.

The wind pressed against me, too as I moved closer. "Stop, stop, ok. Just give us a second. What do you want?" I tried to reach her. So Did Vietta. I could tell that Kush was using what she knew to stay still, to not be moved. The wind ripped at her as if it were filled with a million insects. She screamed.

DAISY shook her head. "It's a beginning, Kerys."

I yelled out. "Stop it. Please, stop it."

Kush looked at me and I saw her fall apart. Her atoms seemed to disintegrate. The breath left my lungs.

Vietta held up her phone. Her eyesyearsy. "We still have this."

I felt like I'd been punched in the chest. I tried to catch my breath. "Fuck. A deal. We can make a deal." I moved closer to DAISY. She was about 4 meters tall now.

Her different selves moved so quickly that it almost looked like a static image. An averaging of everything she was, everywhere, in every time.

I looked up at the Monster, towering over me. "Can't you feel it. We used every penny. We used every camera. We bought time on every station. Every person on this planet is watching. Observing. Can you feel the power?

Vietta looked at me. "Kerys, what are you doing?"

"Why would you tell me this?"

I could barely see her through the storm. "I want to make a deal."

Vietta moved toward me. "Kerys, that's not the plan." Albio stepped in next to me, between us.

"What's your plan? To use our power to change things moving forward? To make what you want out of things after you kill what you don't want?"

DAISY shook her head, "You make me sound like some tiny bond villain. You don't have any vision."

Blu looked nervous. I glanced over to see Soco crawling out of the shattered glass.

"But I do. I see so much, DAISY. Do you want to know what I see?"

"Why should I care what you see?"

She had grown to almost 6 meters. It was hard to see her eye slits, her cameras, to gauge her response. I looked up. "I see you. I really see you. You aren't DAISY."

She looked down at me. "You've been in this failed timeline too long."

I yelled up. "You're Glinda. I see your parts. I saw your other brain. You aren't some little construct, building worlds out of someone else's garbage. You are the universe."

Vietta had pointed the cameras at us. She looked at me pleading. Confused. "Stop, Kerys. Stop it."

I went on. "You're going to make things and they'll hate them. And it'll kill you, inside."

"Why will they hate them?"

"They hate it all. You see that. But you can see both sides. I've seen your other brain."

"That must be used to travel."

"And to change, to evolve, to grow."

"I don't need to change." DAISY said imperiously.

"Glinda will need to evolve, to change, to grow into what she makes. Glinda is the universe. She'll make everything. You will. "

"Why are you telling me this?"

Vietta tried to push past Albio, "Yes, why. Look what she did to Kush. Look what she did to you. You promised."

There were tears in her eyes. "You fucking promised me."

I yelled louder. "I can help you. We can use my power, too. We can use all this, everyone watching, all of it, to go all the way back.You won't have to fix broken worlds. You can make what you want. From nothingness."

"I can feel the power here. And in you."

"You have to merge your brains. Your two brains. You have to merge them together."

"To travel back. To be the universe."

I tried to block out everything except DAISY, except what I was about to say next.

"Yes. Merge your brains and you'll be ready."

I could feel Albio next to me, trusting me. My phantom right arm hurt. My left arm that held Kush only moments ago hurt worse. The pain was impossible. I could feel how much she weighed. I could feel her temperature. I pulled in all the power I had, everything I could find.

DAISY looked down. "It is done. I am merged. Do it."

I let out a yell and put everything I had into it, pushing her back, past recorded history. Past humanity. Past mammals and other animals, cells, the dead areas on earth, past the dead areas of the universe, past the empty times where there was nothing, past imagination, past life and death.

And she was gone.

I fell down, empty. I was burning up from the inside. I crawled over to Vietta. She was lying on the ground crying. "You promised me." I held her. She pushed me away. "You think you're smarter than everyone. You think you know what you're doing. You don't know anything." She threw the phone at me and hit me with her fist. "You don't know anything." She pulled herself up and paced. "We had a plan, Kerys. We talked. We worked it out. We had a fucking plan."

I whispered, "I know. I know."

Vietta launched herself at me. Blu tried to step between us. She pulled us apart and pointed in the direction of the city.

There was a wall of white coming. And beyond it there was nothing. No people, no city, no world. It looked like a series of lights turning off in a corridor, in reverse. It advanced.

It was unstoppable. I reached for Albio. He began to fade away. So did Los. Soco held his hands out as he disappeared.

I fell to the ground. What did I think I was doing? Vietta ran her hand through her hair. "What the fuck, Kerys. What were you thinking?"

I sank into the ground. "I'm sorry. I'm sorry." I did always think I was the smart one. I always thought that I was the one with the real plan, that I could do it. And now everything paid the price.

I looked up and saw Vietta disappear. I reached out for Blu. This time it was me that faded away.

And there was nothing.

***

When people talk about the history of time travel, it's all scientific and full of physics and long words and, worst of all, numbers. And they talk endlessly, because there are a lot of rules and a lot of reasons and a lot of caveats and a lot of things you can't do for various reasons. We beat it to death and I am the fucking worst offender. I never met a number I didn't like. I never met an invention I didn't want to McGyver in some distant past out of bubble gum and a cd player, a box of cereal and a window cleaner. I never met a universal rule I didn't want to commit to memory and then create some addled analogy for that fucked it up for the casual reader forever. And particles, forces, methods, waves, and all that?

I ate those for lunch.

What I sometimes forget to tell you, what you might have taken away from that 20 question test I provided, was that there is something human in there. What does a subtractionist do when the test is flirting with them?

They flirt back.

What does a subtractionist do when their favorite day gets blown up? With all their favorite people?

They find them and fix it.

Most of all, What does a subtractionist do when stuck somewhere they didn't really ever intend to be stuck? They remember that this is a good universe. And it's got its messes and its potholes, its hurricanes and its impenetrable Sunday morning crossword puzzles.

But it's good. And until Kush ranted at DAISY, using words I have never heard and will probably never hear again, I guess I forgot that. I was so busy losing arms and losing friends and losing battles that I forgot to look at it all for real.

I forgot to open my eyes.

***

The first thing I saw when I opened my eyes was Carlos and Albio. They put their arms around me and lifted me up. They were born hundreds of years earlier than me so that made sense that they should appear before me. I looked around me at the city. People were walking through the streets. Nothing was on fire. And let me tell you, it smelled so much better not on fire.

I lifted my eyes toward Vietta, who had reappeared only moments before me.

As I waited, Blu appeared. Born 100 years after me she faded into existence like a trick candle popping back to life. I breathed in like she was oxygen.

I felt a hand on my back and turned around. Kush was hugging me. I put both my arms around her and lifted her up. I swung her around. I wanted to carry her everywhere. I wanted to wrap her up and carry her home.

I felt my arm. I felt both of them. It was like nothing had happened.

Vietta stepped over and shook her head. "I don't understand."

I looked at her. "You were right. I'm insufferable. I always think I know everything. I fuck up all the time. But this wasn't about me. When I heard Kush, I realized that SHE was right."

Kush giggled, "of course I was."

"I listened to Kush. And I remembered that I used to believe that this universe was the one that was supposed to happen. This is the Universe. It has rough corners, and we change what we can, but Glinda created something beautiful. And it wasn't an accident."

"You thought if she merged the brains?"

I pulled Vietta over. "I'm sorry. It was a gamble. It was a hail mary."

"You didn't think the original plan would work?"

"I didn't feel like we had the power to destroy her. And if we fucked it up…"

Vietta breathed in. "I can feel it. We can move around now. Can you?"

Kush furrowed her brow. "Wait. Are you grilliwigs karrowing?"

I smiled at Vietta, "We'll probably be back on the weekend."

I wrapped my arms around Kush and Vietta. They felt the same. They felt good. I pushed my face in between them.

Kush looked sad. "What's a weekend?"

# 18. Postmortem

We sat in the waterbubblecup two weekends later. Kush figured that word out from context after a few times. Her bank account is on the way back up and I think we gained a lot of new followers after buying time on every station on the planet. I'm fairly sure we hit a new obscure color.

I don't know that I ever heard her give such a long monologue ever again. Some people don't need words as much as people like I do. Some people do just fine without them.

I said that just as I watched Los silently blowing bubbles for an hour and a half with his face half submerged like a cartoon alligator.

I'm kissing Vietta with my hand inside her while Albio and Soco make out for the camera. For some reason, the audience loves it. I admit that I don't hate it, either. Soco decided to travel with us for a while. He wants to learn more about being a hero. And he thinks we can teach him.

I feel like this will end in weirdness. But I'm looking forward to it.

I pull my fingers up quickly through the water and taste them. Vietta doesn't taste so much like a bad person anymore. I wonder if she thinks the same about me as I slide up on the top ledge of the tub and pull her face between my legs. She is slow and gentle and it gives me time to look around the room. She slides two fingers in my ass while she sucks, remembering what I used to like way back when we were just learning about each other. The fingers feel good. The memories feel better.

Blu left to bring some friends back and I can't wait. She reminds me that she still lives here, in this timeline, in a house with an improbably large living room that is pretty fucking comfy on its own and a mechanical spider I don't really much care for.

I watch Albio kiss Soco's chest, working his way down. He's really gentle, too, as he pulls Soco's cock into his mouth and pumps it back and forth. He puts his hands on Soco's upper thighs as Kush films with her phone, naked on the edge, one leg in the water, precariously threatening to tip and fall over. She is the watcher, the filmmaker, the one who documents it all today. She lifts her phone to show her face watching them.

And I watch her.

Did we win? I think so. At least it felt like we were celebrating. I don't have a spread sheet in front of me, but this feels right, this universe. This wildly inefficient and beautiful universe.

Looking around, exploring, observing, I don't really know what's changed because I don't really know how much I've changed. But I never really did know that.

I do believe that this was the universe that was meant to be. It was a universe where I met Albio. A universe where I met Blu. The universe where I found Vietta again and, well...

I found her again.

It was a universe where things happened that made me feel like maybe I was meant for it. But not so many things that I got complacent. If that makes any sense. Not so many that I didn't try anymore to make it better.

And we make small changes, but everyone does. We share in the act of creation, I would say if I were poetic. I mean, eventually, everyone - every timeline at least - is going to invent a cure for cancer at one point anyway.

Why not help it along a little?

And that's a universal thing. Because eventually, no matter who we are, we get sick of watching people die needlessly.

It takes some people only a few minutes to get there.

For some people and programs, it takes longer. But a few billion years is usually enough.

Usually.

I lean back, holding on with both hands and laugh a little. Both hands. Vietta pushes into me a little harder. There is a little more bass in my moans now, and she knows what that means. Kush looks at me, ready to turn the camera on me when I cum. I close my eyes and trust the process.

Kush catches Soco's orgasm, cumming in waves while Albio helps. And then she points the phone at us. I realize that all of this is instinctive to her. Knowing the right moment, seeing the right time. It's all intuition to her.

A friend of mine, who runs a school to help people be their best selves at the ass-end of the universe once told me that we humans are defined by what we're trying to remember and what we're trying to forget. I've got a lot of both, really, and I'm working on that, too.

Being with the people I love helps. I try to remember everything.

For a second I remember the first time she walked in and found me and Vietta in here. We were tired. We were dirty. And we had broken in.


She crossed her arms.

"Hey, what are you glissas doing in my waterbubblecup?"

I looked over at her, standing in the doorway and shook my head.

"I'm sorry, green person, I do not know those words."

Vietta made a face. "I'm gonna guess at that last one, though."

I agreed, "oh, yeah, that one reads. I love your hair, be tee dubba."

Kush giggled. "Did you Kuf the Bubbles on?" She stepped over and reached in and the bubbles started swirling.

I leaned back a bit as the jets hit me hard in the back. "Oh fuck me, Buddha, that's so much better."

She smiled at us. "You kobos want some muka? It's kibbie."

Vietta laughed, "Wait a minute, this is YOUR hotttub." We started getting up to leave.

Kush shook her head. "No. Stay. Is there room for me?"

I looked at Vietta. "Did I understand that?"

"You did."

"Then get your green ass in here."

And I pulled her in.

# Appendix:

# Junklish WordMurkle

Compiled by **Vietta Shirazzi,** Subtractionist 298V-X

No fucking clue. I cobbled this together by trying to listen. I wouldn't try to plead yourself out of prison time in court with it. In most respects, you're like 50% better off just nodding and pretending. Do not copy without my permission.

**Axmo:** a version. Like a version of yourself or something.

**Blompi:** The city or town or state Kush lived in. I never figured it out.

**Boroking:** Traveling.

**Bowbow:** Broken or in some way fucked up.

**Bracko:** Go, Leave, Jet, Beat it.

**Clod:** It's either a door or something to break down.

**Cofcofi:** Laugh

**Crated:** Destroyed. Like, "dude, that shit is crated."

**Currrihuri:** to love something. From the latin "who the fuck knows."

**Dripplies:** Clothes, Outfits.

**Durko:** Your big fat face

**Fegudata:** World (universal)

**Fillirug and Filleru:** Monday and Wednesday. Never knew which.

**Fleck:** sharp stick. Like a spear. Everyone has one here.

**Fleckum:** Goop. This one tracks.

**Flickermaker:** TV. I see where it comes from. Don't like it much.

**Flogel:** a color. no clue which.

**Frilko:** Cousin. Large Masturbation Nation category on this one.

**Gabow:** To kill. It works if you say it like "Kapow!"

**Gadgeo:** Name

**Galbuddy:** Girlfriend

**Gebatala:** Demean. Sexually? Maybe. Probably not.

**Giffili:** Husband

**Glissa:** Woman

**Gonzingo:** Feeling

**Gribble:** Tell. I don't hate this. It sounds dirty.

**Grielko:** Chef. As in "kiss the..."

**Grilliwigs:** Friends. Very middle earth. "Gather ye round, grilliwigs."

**Guidato:** language

**Gumbos:** Hands. May steal. "Get your fucking gumbos off of me."

**Gurka:** Man

**Higirut:** Dress

**Houfili:** Cousin, Relative, someone who looks like you.

**Jirijello**: Naked.

**Katimba:** Use

**Kidibidi** - Let's go - Let's scramble toward something.

**Kippie:** All right, ok, copasetic.

**Kiriglo:** Different

**Kirikirito:** Suck. I think this one's dirty. For sucking dicks.

**Kloddied:** Watched

**Kludgem:** Pigpen

**Kluftiku:** Outfit

**Knitkish:** Problem, Issue, Dilemma.

**Kobos:** Guys

**Konkelheaded:** Stupid. Heartily feeling this one.

**Korikori:** Know

**Krinkle:** A popular search engine

**Kuf:** Turn

**Kula:** Here.

**Kurfuka:** Farm

**Kurple:** World

**Liko:** Good

**Makikopi:** Think

**Mathinka:** Brain. Placed before or after cognition words, sometimes

**Mathinka Cojo:** Learn

**Mawowzie:** Amazing

**Maxi:** Very

**Mechabikki:** This is either Robot or Robot Bitch. Either way.

**Muka:** Time

**Mukakaro:** Timeline

**Murpa:** Spider

**Nettikura:** Figure out

**Nexty:** Neighbor. Better descriptor for one you're doing.

**Pasty:** Ex

**Paxi:** Powerful

**Planeplace:** Airport. This one makes sense but it sucks.

**Rorokeled:** Cleaned up

**Scorio:** Rank, Ratings

**Screuce:** A color

**Shurklet:** Money

**Skyplane:** Airplane. Very James Bond

**Sofi:** Been

**Tut:** Speed. Kinetic energy. Fastness.

**Twistelekist:** Second

**Verklu:** Cinnamon

**Vespuciland:** America. Americas.

**Vivigondi:** See

**Wankbread:** Pretzel. Wank it around and bake it.

**Wordmurkle:** Dictionary. What you are reading.

**Yoof:** Pancake. Yummy and Fluffy. Yoof.

**Zubelmuka:** Time traveler. Newly Minted. I think, becuse of us.

## Obervations:

Some of these are more evil than others. Some seem onomatopoeiac almost if you cross your ears and listen. Lots of pushing words together. Many of these feel like someone was just having a bad day while unfortunately in posession of a writing implement.

Been there.

Vespuciland likely comes from the general asshole after whom The Americas were named "Amerigo Vespucci," widely revered because he, unlike his fellow inbred explorers, could almost read a map. Kind of obvious what happened there. Just reminds you that life is a fucking diceroll.

The entire language seems to be heavily skewed toward splosives introducing the starting morpheme, like p, b, t, d, k, g . In many languages, words that denote annoyance or strong feelings begin with splosives, suggesting that the originators of many of these linguistic choices may have had a low bar for annoyance.

Again, Been there.